The Step Doctors

by

J.D. GRAYSON

25,000 words

CONTENTS

THE STEP DOCTORS

CHAPTER ONE...7

CHAPTER TWO 28

CHAPTER THREE 55

CHAPTER FOUR 85

CHAPTER FIVE 102

THE STEP DOCTORS 2: SEEDED BY A STEP

CHAPTER ONE..120

CHAPTER TWO..146

CHAPTER THREE 165

CHAPTER FOUR..194

CHAPTER FIVE 211

OTHER BOOKS BY J.D. GRAYSON 240

ABOUT J.D. GRAYSON...248

All books are now available in Paperback. For autographed copies please send your request to JDGrayson@hotmail.com

Visit J.D. Grayson's website to signup for a new release alerts.

Website: www.JDGraysonBooks.com

Twitter: @JDGraysonBooks

CHAPTER ONE

Darcy Smith entered her stepfather's medical practice. The curvy redhead approached the office sign-in sheet. Before she could write her name, the receptionist said, "Family doesn't need to sign in or wait, Ms. Abel..."

"Actually...it's Ms. Smith...remember? I'm the stepdaughter and stepsister of the doctors," she said with blushing cheeks. "I guess that makes them my...step-doctors." Currently 18, but having lived with the two men since age 4, she saw them as family. Though such an admittance made her feel like an orphan.

"Right, I'm sorry," the receptionist corrected. "Having known you since childhood, I always forget you're not blood relation. Step or not...go on inside."

*****

Darcy was brought back to an exam room, a gyno chair awaited. The nurse handed her a gown. "Remove all your clothing, underwear and bra included. Put on the gown cover...have a seat. The doctor will be in soon, Ms. Abel."

"Smith. I'm Ms. Smith," she reminded the nurse.

"Oh right, we just know you as the doctor's family," she said, exiting the room.

The redheaded Darcy exhaled, waiting to see the medical group's female doctor. Although her stepfather was the OB-GYN of the group, she only saw the practice's feminine representation. It was the rule set by the senior doctor: neither he nor his General Practitioner son could examine her. It was the first time Darcy's matured body would be exposed to another. The mere thought made her heart race.

It could be worse, she thought. *It could be a man seeing my body...touching my lady lumps. It could be my stepfather or even...stepbrother! OMG...that would be gross!* Having two doctors in her direct family, she gladly took the free medical care. She'd never dared to imagine either familial doctor examining her. *I'd be so embarrassed! Stepbrother Sean hasn't seen me naked since walking in on me changing. And that was a mistake...at least I think it was. I wasn't as boobalicious back then...as I am now!*

Darcy felt her nipples stiffen, making the medical gown rise. A tingling crawled through her body, confusing her thoroughly. *Umm...why exactly did that just happen? And why did it feel...sorta...good?* She wondered, having never had an orgasm to know the difference.

Although the step-doctors weren't unattractive to her eyes, it was limited to a role-model sort of way. Any fantasy featuring steps was banned from her mind. Societal taboos strictly set the rules for her. Even with no official relations, such thoughts were unacceptable. No matter what came naturally, fear of judgment assured her denial.

Just chill, Darcy, she instructed herself. *That won't happen. The female doctor will be in soon, no step worries.* Knowing she was safe from such an embarrassing fate, she set her mind on the exam to come. She had no idea what would be done to her, but she imagined it would be *invasive* at best.

A knock sounded on the door, followed by a white-coated *man*. "Oh shit...I mean, oh...Sean," she shouted in shock. Her stepbrother, Dr. Sean Abel entered the room. He was 30-years-old, broad shouldered, dark-haired and 6'1. He'd only been a practicing doctor for a year. Having never seen him wear the white doctor-coat before, she found herself ogling him, oddly breathless by the sight.

"Step-sis," he said, hugging her in the gyno chair. Her barely covered body pressed against his strong chest.

"Are you supposed to hug patients? Isn't that...like...wrong...or something?"

He disengaged, "You're correct...I probably should address you as Ms. Smith too. *Step-sis* isn't quite professional. However, I think our secret's safe," he said with a wink.

Secret? What secret? She silently wondered. *Did he mean the name thing...or like...other things to come? Relax, he's just here to say hi.* "Thanks for checking on me," she said.

"Oh...the nurse didn't tell you?"

She remained quiet for a while. "Uh...tell me *what* exactly?"

"Dr. Richards is out...I'll be your doctor today."

A massive gasp filled Darcy's 18-year-old lungs. She could barely breathe. "I...I...I..."

"Are you OK?" he asked, moving toward his stepsister. Placing a hand over her heart, his touch rested between her natural C-cups. "Your heart's racing."

"Just...a little nervous," she managed to speak.

"*That's* normal," he said, removing his hand from her heart area. He studied her medical chart as his eyes opened wide. "I see you're having lower abdominal and...*vaginal* pain!" Dr. Sean Abel's face was the red one now. Having not prescreened Darcy's chart, he was taken by surprise. Of course, he could've read it, like he did all the other patients. It was as if he didn't want a reason to deny her. Though more likely, it was *himself* he didn't want to deny.

Despite a direct order not to examine her, something inside him begged to take Darcy on. Sean couldn't even explain it. It was like a piece of forbidden fruit, hanging before him. However, the reality of the moment suddenly hit, *Stepsister plus vaginal exam equals...holy shit. I haven't seen her nude since...oh fuck yes! Those breasts are even bigger now! Stay professional, you're a doctor, damn it!*

Darcy's red cheeks matched the fiery tone of her hair. "My va-jay-jay is suddenly feeling better...I'm cured," she said, holding her medical gown closed, attempting to get up.

"Sit back down, Ms. Smith," Sean's doctor voice suddenly emerged, bold and authoritative.

The mere sound made her sink back into the gyno chair. While growing up, she was always submissive to the men in the house, but something about that white coat made her melt into submission. "Yes, sir," she responded, telling herself, *Did I really just call my stepbrother, sir? Could this get any weirder?*

"Before the examination, I'm going to do a scan."

"Scan? Not in one of those...tube thingies...right?"

"Yes."

"Does it matter that I'm claustrophobic?"

"It won't bother me at all," he joked.

*****

Dr. Sean Abel led his stepsister into the scan room. The redhead gasped upon sight of the MRI machine. The scan tube went body-length deep, able to house a tall person. At 5'3, Darcy would be swallowed inside. "It's like a coffin! I'll suffocate in there!"

"You'll be fine. You're 18, an adult now...you can handle it. Follow me," he ordered, leading her to the MRI bed. A black male MRI tech joined him. Dr. Abel patted the surface.

"Can I go in on my hands and knees...so I can crawl out if I need to?" she asked.

"No. Lay on your back...the machine will do the rest," he said with a smile.

She nervously exhaled, creeping towards the plush cushion like a bed of nails. Holding her gown closed tightly, she quickly lay flat, stiffer than rigor mortis. As the tech pushed a few buttons, Dr. Sean

Abel said, "Once you're secure, we'll exit to the observation room...behind glass."

"You're not staying with me?" she asked in a trembling voice.

"The radiation exposure isn't recommended."

"Then shouldn't I come with you? I mean, it's not recommended for me either."

"Not recommended...for those *not* getting scanned. You'll be fine, I promise," he said.

"All set," the MRI tech announced.

"OK, before you go in...I'm going to need the symptomatic area exposed."

Darcy turned a deeper shade of red, staring down at the short medical gown's edge. *No way!* She thought. *I got an idea.* "I'll just spread the gown at the stomach area, holding the bottom closed."

"But what about the vaginal pain? I need to scan that too."

"Just forget I ever said that," she begged.

"No need to be bashful," Sean said, trying to conceal the growing arousal in his mind and pants. Removing his stepsister's hand blockade, he parted her gown at the hips. Like a flaming beacon of lust, a bed of red pubic hair stared back. Another idea silently struck him. *OK, I know this is unethical...career ending with anyone but family...but with Darcy...I can get away with this. How many times will I have a chance to shave my stepsister? Never again. Damn it...I'm doing it.* "Ahh, *that's* going to be an issue," he announced.

Both the tech and Darcy looked surprised. "My vagina?" she asked.

"Your pubic hair."

"Really?" she asked.

"Since when?" the tech joined in simultaneously.

Communicating with a hard stare, Sean Abel spoke to the tech in silent man-code. "Since my stepsister's health is very important to me...I must get accurate results!" he said in an overly dramatic sales pitch.

The African-American tech nodded, known for his own unethical moves over the years. "Right...family *comes* first around here."

"Please retrieve an electric razor," Sean requested.

"My pleasure, doctor!" the tech said enthusiastically, anxiously awaiting the show. He ran with vigor to get the razor, as Darcy sat in disbelief. *Is my stepbrother really gonna shave me? I've never even shaved it before...I gotta make a run for it.*

Before she could escape, the breathless tech returned. "One electric buzzer, doctor."

"Thank you," Dr. Abel said, as both men snapped on a pair of fresh latex gloves. The black tech placed his hand under Darcy's juicy butt cheeks, lifting her. As extra paper lining was added, she was further exposed to them.

Next, Dr. Abel leaned inward, placing his fingers upon Darcy's vaginal lips. Slightly squeezing them together, he trimmed the red pubes. Beginning at the lower abdomen, he mowed thick strands of bright red hair to the ground. Using the razor's lowest setting, pale bare skin remained in his wake.

The tech collected hair clumps, clearing them away. The buzzing continued near Darcy's clit, making her squirm from the rumbling tickle between her legs. She watched her stepbrother wield the razor in dominant doctor fashion. A sudden sexual fire stung her. Quickly looking away, she thought, *Oh no, you won't go there! No horniness allowed!*

The sensation only increased with each stroke. Finally, the buzzing stopped. A wet paper towel rinsed her off, followed by a dry one. "All clean and ready to scan," Sean announced, knowing that full heads of hair were scanned everyday. *It was worth every risk,* he assured himself.

What will it look like? One of those...bald cats? It must be so ugly now! Darcy wondered, slowly peering downward. To her shock, a smooth, neat and sexy sight stared back. *Is it wrong that I think...it's actually kinda hot looking?* She wondered, seeing her lips and protruding clit exposed freely.

Before she could think on it any further, Dr. Sean Abel announced, "Now, just shut your eyes, hold still...it'll be over before you know it," he instructed.

With one press of a button, the MRI bed began retreating inward. The curvy redheaded patient was barely beyond her shoulders when panic enveloped her. "It's like being buried alive!" she shouted, her head rising upward toward the tube's low-hanging, arched top.

Dr. Abel dove to stop her, pinning his stepsister flat to the MRI bed. Still outside the tube, Darcy's smooth legs flailed and kicked wildly. Her smooth pussy was further exposed to the tech, whose black hands trapped the patient's thighs in place.

Nearly inside the tube with her, Darcy's stepbrother rested upon her barely covered C-cups. He could feel her hard nipples poking through his white coat. "Relax!"

"Get me outta here!" she cried.

Dr. Sean Abel was face to face with his redheaded stepsister. He could smell her sweet breath, cherry-flavored from the gum she had recently chewed. Her innocent tears, youthful vulnerability made him harder than he already was.

"Strap her down!" Sean Abel shouted. He yanked a black strap from the table's side, pulling it across Darcy's throbbing chest. Aligning it perfectly with her covered-breasts, the strap inverted the thick red nipples with teasing pressure. He buckled it into the MRI bed's opposite end, trapping her arms.

Next, he moved down to her waist, unveiling another strap. Yanking it outward from the MRI bed, he draped it across her hips, locking it on the opposite side. Partly brushing his stepsister's swollen clit, any movement she made would stimulate her.

However, a sweet scent suddenly struck his nose. He stared down, seeing beads of satisfaction trickle down her leg. As scared as she was, her arousal was heightened by fear itself. *She's turned on,* he silently thought. *Is it me who's turning her on...or just the situation? Should I venture further in the pleasure department than planned? Do I dare make her cum during the exam? Shit, what if she tells dad? I can't believe I'm thinking this!*

Simultaneously, the black MRI tech removed a strap, lining it over Darcy's thick upper thighs. He also noticed the storm of feminine rain drizzling from her snatch. Finally, he locked her ankles in-place. "She's secure...ready to send her deeper in," the tech announced, placing his finger on the entrance button.

"Wait," Dr. Sean Abel announced, still hearing slight sobs sound from his stepsister. Removing his latex glove, he reached for her captive hand, holding it gently. She suddenly stopped crying, staring outward at her stepbrother. His mere touch appeared to calm her. The reaction was unexpected and mysterious. "Continue on."

"You're really staying?" she asked, as the tech sent her deeper into the tube. Her vagina and abdomen were in the scan zone.

"I am," Sean said, sailing partially inside with her.

"But...the radiation," she said.

"A risk I'm willing to take for my...stepsister," the doctor declared.

"Have fun," the tech said, heading behind the glass barrier. Darcy remained fixed upon her stepbrother's eyes, in awe of his sacrifice. She barely noticed her surroundings until the scan was over.

Dr. Abel unstrapped Darcy, freeing her from the machine. He said, "Now it's time to examine you."

The entranced girl suddenly stiffened again, returning to reality.

*****

Darcy waited nervously in the gyno chair. Her thoughts consisted of one repeated sentence. *My stepbrother just saw my lady lips!*

Dr. Sean Abel entered with a scan in-hand, "Good news. Nothing abnormal in the MRI."

"Vag-tastic! So no need to examine me! See ya!" she said, attempting to quickly exit the chair.

Nudging her back into the seat, he said, "Don't be ridiculous, Darcy. The pain you're feeling is concerning. At your age...that shouldn't be happening. Before I examine you gynecologically, let me ask a few questions."

"Vagina questions?"

"Something like that. So, is the pain constant?"

She thought long and hard, *Do I answer honestly? I could give answers that steer him away from my bad place...but then I still have the pain. I'll be short in my answers...no dirty details.* "Nope."

"It's only occasional."

"Yup."

"That's good. Is there any particular activity or certain time of day you feel it?"

"Umm...the timing just depends."

"On what?"

"My mood."

The look on his face was one of confusion. "Answer my first question."

"I forgot it already."

"A particular activity that triggers the pain?"

"You mean like...while doing homework?"

"If that homework involves the vagina...sure."

Her face soured, *Oh just tell him already. Get it over-with!* "Maybe the pain comes...while...touching *it*."

Dr. Abel's eyes opened wide, "Now we're getting to the issue. Please elaborate on that touching. Washing it in the shower? Putting on your underwear? *Insertion*."

"Kinda," she said, blushing deeply.

"Which one?"

"The last one."

"Insertion. No need to be shy...masturbating is completely normal. A girl your age is just learning about herself...about pleasure. Do you touch yourself often?"

Darcy's face turned so red, it was crimson. "Can we just use that other word? It's less creepy, more doctorish."

"Insertion?"

"Yeah."

"Well, it depends on what's being inserted...who's doing the insertion."

Oh shit, no! She thought. "Fine! I finger myself...jeez!"

"Relax...this information won't leave the room. Remember, I'm here to help you as a doctor...not judge you as a stepbrother."

His words didn't change her embarrassment level. "Are we done?"

"We've only started, relax. So how many times a day?"

She exhaled, "A few."

"A few as in two? Is three times the charm?"

Darcy's exhale increased. "In my pants...five, sometimes...seven," she said in humiliation.

Son of a bitch...my stepsister's horny! Sean Abel shouted to himself. "Ok...one finger or multiple?"

"One...is enough. In fact, even that's a bit too much."

"Elaborate."

"Well, that's kinda my problem. One finger hurts a little...any more hurt...bad. I think I'm broken."

Dr. Abel smiled, starting to understand the issue. "I'd venture you never orgasmed."

"I don't know."

"You'd know if you orgasmed, trust me. So no larger attempts...like a dildo or vibrator?"

"No way!"

"Non-plastic items...such as...a penis?"

Darcy looked toward the floor, mumbling, "*Virgin.* That makes me like 90 years old in classmate years. Such a loser."

"Not at all. In fact, if you saw what I've seen lately...you'd be proud not to be a walking VD."

"Huh?"

"Never mind. Let me examine you and we'll get to the root of your problem, ok?"

"I guess," she said.

"Just put your feet in the stirrups like this," he said, taking hold of his stepsister's feminine feet, lifting them upward. The chair automatically reclined, leaving Darcy on her back. Each ankle was secured into the stirrup cuff, sweet pink slit spread wide and wet.

After slapping on a new pair of latex gloves, he studied his stepsister in the gyno-chair. Thankful for his loose-fitting medical coat, his erection remained hidden. He thought, *I must feel those boobs!* Stepping between her smooth thighs, he announced, "I'm going to examine your breasts first."

"But they don't hurt."

"It's just procedure...part of the exam," he said, placing rubber hands at her gown's mid-part. Spreading the gown between the breasts, he unveiled his stepsister's C-cups like priceless art.

With every exposed inch, the curvy redhead was more vulnerable. Chills crossed her porcelain skin, air-conditioned breeze nipped at her freckles. Both the right and left breasts were revealed at once.

I'm practically naked in front of my stepbrother! Darcy's thoughts raced as quickly as her heart beat. As odd as she felt, every erogenous zone throbbed with taboo pleasure. When Dr. Abel grasped her right breast, it tingled even greater. His fingers squeezed the bulbous base, engorging it from the back. Each fingertip pressed, while his palm massaged. Encircling the feminine sphere, he choked it, checking for lumps around her nubile knobs.

The redhead's curvy body stiffened, hands grasped the chair's armrests. Every inch closer to nipple contact, the sexy stepsister squirmed more. She'd never imagined a rough handling of her mammaries hurting so good. Though nothing compared to his pinching of her areola.

Feeling her nipple grow between his fingertips, Sean Abel squeezed the sensitive red dart. One latex hand remained choking the C-cup breast base. Turning to a pinch, he slowly began tugging at her tip, performing a milking motion. Testing her nipple sensitivity he heard her breath thicken, slight moans sneak out. Although she didn't realize it, Darcy's eyes slowly rolled upward, drifting into an undiscovered world of pleasurable pain.

He switched to the left breast, performing an even harder exam. At one point, the redhead's pale skin turned purple, engorged from the choking swell of commanding hands. Milking her nipple more aggressively, he yanked the thick, inch-long treat further from its puffed base. Darcy's body shook from the sensation, her leg brushing the step-doctor's hard cock.

"They feel wonderful...in a healthy...professional manner, of course," Dr. Sean Abel said, removing his C-cup hold.

Snapping back to reality, Darcy's modest embarrassment returned. Pulling her gown closed, she declared, "Since you don't need my boobs anymore..."

"I need them!" Dr. Abel insisted, spreading the gown back open. "The gown gets in the way...I need to observe...everything," he said. Sean pulled up a rolling chair, sitting between Darcy's moist slit.

The scent of her sweet arousal struck his desperate senses. Not only was it greater than inside the MRI tube, it was greater than any woman he'd ever inhaled. Leaning as closely into her as possible, he thought, *If I could bottle this up, I'd quit air itself.* Forcing himself to focus, his eyes targeted a beautiful sight. Rimming the tight ring around the vaginal entrance, he announced, "Your hymen's still intact."

"Hymen?"

"You might know it as your...un-popped cherry?"

"Ah, I've heard that saying before. Yeah, well, as I said...I'm a virgin."

"Some rupture during masturbation...I'll be extra careful not to tear it. Doctor or not, the last thing you need is your stepbrother popping your cherry," he joked, as the two suddenly caught eyes. Sean saw Darcy's nipples stiffen even more. His words clearly turned her on.

"Gross!" she shouted, not realizing her guilt by bodily reaction.

Moving forward, Dr. Abel squirted lube on a thin metal tube. Spreading her sweetness further, he placed it to her sticky hole. "This is thin, guaranteed not to make you bleed," he said confidently.

"Bleed?"

"Cherry pop," he said, informing her what to expect someday.

"Hearing it put like that...I'm not sure I ever wanna lose it," she said.

"Don't worry, it'll all be worth it...once the right man is inside you," he said boldly.

The confident words made Darcy's body tingle. *Stop tingling!* She told herself silently. "Woooo!" she shouted, reacting to a difference sensation altogether. It was painful. The steel scope barely touched the curvy redhead's lips. It hadn't even entered her yet.

Dr. Abel continued onward, sliding it into her creamy canal. Noting her mental discomfort, he refused to stop. Darcy's body stiffened more, thighs tightened. Prevented from entering deeper, pressure was evident in the scope sluggishness. *Vaginismus...caused by fear,* he silently diagnosed her.

Realizing the tension was subconscious, he ordered, "Bear down...push like you're having a bowel movement," he instructed. She grunted, as he spread her extra wide. The action made her naturally widen more, forcing the scope to go deeper. The metal invader touched her cervix wall. Darcy quickly tightened again.

The doctor unscrewed a metal cap from the scope's outer end. An illuminated blanket of velvet flesh was magnified through glass. A pristine Promised Land awaited, untouched and unspoiled by mankind. Her tiny cervical ring was present. Pressing a button, Sean pierced the ring with an attached probe. It pushed the tip through the cervix opening.

A deep moan sounded from the redheaded stepsister. She wiggled in sync with the probe inside her womb. Clear liquid leaked from the cervix, as Darcy's heavy breaths matched the pressure inside her. As painful as it was, for the first time, she felt a twinge of pleasure accompany penetration. Deep inside, she denied it was Sean causing it.

As Dr. Sean Abel removed the scope, Darcy exhaled deeply. Her hymen was still intact. The step-doctor said, "Your canal's healthy."

"So am I just a quack? Is it all in my head?"

"Not so fast, Darcy. It's much more complicated than that. You have *Vaginismus.*"

"Vagi...what?"

23

"In laymen's terms...you're tightening your vaginal muscles. Subconsciously, of course."

"I know it's tightening. I was kinda hoping...you could tell me how to fix it."

"Well, with nothing physically wrong...the problem is mental."

"I knew it! Lock me up...I'm a nut!"

"You're perfectly sane, Darcy. It's just a case of fear. The anticipation of pain causes the pain itself."

"I'm not afraid of my vagina!" she said defensively.

"It's not a conscious thing. Look...let me show you...it'll make more sense." He grabbed a tube of lube, squirting a glob into his latex glove. After each finger was soaked, he spread her lips wider. First he entered one finger, feeling her wet kitty tighten around it. "How's that feel?"

"Hurts...not crazy hurt...but not good."

Placing another finger at her slit, he carefully entered a second digit. She tightened more, body tensing greater from the prior entrance. "Now?"

"It's hurting more."

Adding a third, he walked the risky line of popping her hymen. Darcy grasped the chair's armrests, squeezing. Her feet dug into the stirrups, vaginal muscles choked the three fingers from going deeper. Dr. Abel said, "I needn't ask about that one."

"OK...this isn't telling me something I didn't know, Sean."

"That part's coming," he said, suddenly pinching her clitoris. A massive gasp filled the air, as Darcy's vaginal tension shifted to her abdomen. Dr. Abel's fingers slid deeply to the knuckle. The redhead's sensation went from pain to pure pleasure. However, the moment she refocused, she tightened again. The hurt returned.

"What'd you do?" she asked.

"I stimulated your clitoris. More relevant to your issue...I simply provided a distraction. By causing a surprise...creating a new fear, the vaginal tension shifted."

"OK, but it hurts again. So what now?"

"I want you to touch it yourself."

"What? Here? Now? In front of you?"

"Stop being bashful." He grasped her right hand with his free one. Grasping her clit between two fingers, he asked, "Feel that little button? I want you to pinch it."

After a long pause, she did. Another gasp sounded. Her vaginal tension shifted again, quickly returning afterward. "Pain's back...epic fail, doc."

"Now rub...in small circles," he said, slowly guiding his stepsister's hand in clitoral massage. All the while, Dr. Sean Abel's three fingers remained inside his patient.

With each new clitoral revolution, her vaginal discomfort softened, slowly opening to her stepbrother. The doctor removed his guiding hand from hers, letting her take the reigns. Feeling his fingers get newfound blood flow, he began gently guiding them in a fucking motion. Speaking in a soft whisper, he said, "Good girl. Keep going...you're doing great."

In a near trance, Darcy didn't hear her stepbrother's encouragement. Her clitoral circles picked up pace, pleasure rising with each quickening spin. The doctor's fingers sank deeper into a vaginal expansion, Darcy's swollen button swelled more. She felt a pressure building within, a warmth she'd never know. Orgasm was nearing.

Right before she could fully let go, her eyelids crept open. *OMG, I think I'm about to cum for the first time ever! And...my stepbrother will be the reason! That can't happen. No way...stop now! Think of someone gross...like a bloated Al Gore.* Darcy's hand flew off her clit, her vaginal muscles stiffened again, trapping her stepbrother's hand inside. "It hurts again!"

Not wanting to stop, Dr. Abel ached to make her cum. However, he knew an extended treatment could bring much more than fingering. He even imagined a future exam involving his cock. "It's OK, Darcy. Rome wasn't build overnight," he said, removing his sticky fingers from the redheaded patient. "I'll need you to work on it at home."

"As if I didn't have enough homework," she declared.

"I think this'll be more rewarding than arithmetic," he said. Reaching into a supply drawer, he unveiled a thin rubber dilator. It had a wide round base, insuring it wouldn't get lost inside. Unwrapping the plastic, he handed it to his patient.

"Is this really a...rubber dick?" she asked, holding it like a hot potato.

"In the medical community, we like to use a more professional term. *Dilator*...made to help your muscles adapt to sensation and pressure. It's girth isn't sufficient enough to rupture a hymen, so don't worry."

"When do I put it in?"

"Tonight would be best...sleep with it in. In fact, I need you to leave it in...for two days straight."

She gasped. "But...one of those is a school day!"

"Just take deep breaths...you'll get used to it. If it makes you feel any better...I'll come by tonight...after my last patient. I'll help you with it before bed."

Dizzy with worry, Darcy stared at the rubber phallus in her hands. "Can I even walk with this stuffed inside me?"

"Yes...your Kegel muscles with strengthen as a result. You can get dressed now," he said, heading toward the door. "Oh by the way...tell dad I said hi. We've been too busy to even cross paths in our own practice. By the way...lets keep this appointment between you and me. You know his rule."

Her face cringed as her stepbrother exited. *He just said dad...uh, that gave me the creeps!* Taking another long look at the dilator, she gasped in disbelief.

.

CHAPTER TWO

"Hey, step-dad," Darcy said, entering her attractive home. The redhead hugged the salt and pepper haired, 54-year-old man. Dr. Tim Abel looked a decade younger. All the female patients tried to snag him. However, no one got a second look. His heart beat for one woman alone.

"After all these years, I still can't get you to call me...*dad*?" he asked.

"Sorry," she said, leaving the real reason of refusal to her silent thoughts. *I love him like a real dad...though I just feel strange calling him one. Don't know why?*

The doctor stepfather released a sad sigh. "Can you believe she's been gone 10-years to the day?"

"I try not to think about it much...but I can't seem to forget. No matter how hard I try."

"Never forget your mother," he said. "Whether she's living or dead...she was an amazing woman."

"I'd never forget *her*...I just wish I could forget *that* day. Even though I was only 8 then...I still remember every detail so clearly. The car accident...you telling me. I felt like an orphan."

"And I told you...you'll never be an orphan...never! I meant it then...mean it now," he said powerfully. "Do you understand me?"

"Yes, sir," she said.

"The truth is...the pain will always be with us. Like it or not."

"You're a good doctor. If anyone can find the cure to fix our hearts...*you'll* do it."

Tim Abel unleashed a sad smile, clearly not in agreement. Embracing his stepdaughter, the feeling brought Darcy back to the past. She remembered meeting him for the first time. At the age of 4, the recently divorced doctor entered her life. Within a month, her mother fell in love, marrying the soul mate.

Having been born fatherless, Darcy's deadbeat dad left them penniless and alone. She never knew him. The redhead was delivered into the world, abandoned by man. The good doctor filled that gaping void in the child's heart.

In the present moment, Darcy's stepfather kissed her forehead. He hugged her even tighter, his heart beat against hers. Suddenly feeling an 8-year-old's heart beat as her own, the redhead waded back into a fog of pained youth. She remembered the feeling of that same embrace.

A 20-year-old stepbrother Sean watched beside her. Up to that moment, The older step-sibling was unhappy and untrusting of the redheaded addition. He saw his stepsister as an annoying nuisance.

Not only did Darcy encroach on his space, she was absorbing his father's attention.

Darcy recalled the look in her stepfather's eyes. She could sense something wrong, fearfully awaiting the news. Tim Abel said, "I'm so sorry, Darcy...your mom's been in a car accident."

"She'll be OK...right, step-dad? She's coming home soon?"

A long pause filled the air. "No, baby. She's not."

"Can we visit her...at the hospital?"

"There's no visitation...where she is now."

"Where's that?"

"She's...gone to heaven."

"No!" the young girl screamed. "Mom's don't die! They come home...always come home. She'll come home! I know it!"

He hugged her tighter, feeling the girl cry into his chest. She felt the grown man tremble with pent up rage. Although Tim didn't tell his stepdaughter, it wasn't a natural death that came for his wife, but a careless drunk driver. She was taken instantly, no one got to say goodbye.

The young redhead cried harder, trying to imagine a life without her mother. She felt so lost, so scared. Suddenly, a second pair of arms wrapped around her. Shocked, Darcy turned to see stepbrother Sean showing his love. Up to that point in their step-lives, he was cold to her, stranger-like. They'd lived as siblings for four years, though it wasn't until that moment, encased in the men's arms, she finally felt like family. Even in such horror, they made her feel safe.

Their joint security brought a protection needed for survival. Two human-shields had formed around her shattered heart. On the coldest day of her life, their warmth made her feel like she'd never be alone, blood relations or not.

"Do I have to leave now? Go to another home?" Darcy asked.

"Never!" Stepfather Tim assured her. "This is *your* home! We're your *family*...now and forever! I promise you! You'll never be alone as long as I live."

She turned to her stepbrother. "You'll always be my family too, Sean?"

"I will, step-sis," Sean assured, patting her head. Having always wanted a brother, Darcy remembered feeling like she finally had one.

It was on the worst day of her life, she gained another protector. The older kid who teased and treated her as an outsider, transformed into a loving-dominant as well. Both males dedicated their lives to raising her right.

She recalled the following years, the step's attempt at dating. Though every woman was secondary to Darcy's life. If a woman tried to treat the redhead with disrespect, they were dumped. Any date that got in the way of homework time or a school play, was cancelled. Darcy was their life, their responsibility. At times, it appeared to become competition between father and son. However, the head of the household always won *that* battle. Both remained single to the day.

The bond that formed from loss, linked Darcy to their hearts in an unbreakable way. Just like no woman could compete, no man could ever escape their shadows. In her eyes, everyone else would always be a boy to their manhood. No one could ever bring her the ease she felt on that day. They were her heroes.

Darcy's mind returned to the present moment, she broke the hug. Gazing into each other's blue eyes, they wiped their tears away. "Thank you, step-dad," she said sincerely.

"For what?"

"For loving me...protecting me. For giving me a family."

"You don't have to thank me...for what came naturally. You always were apart of *me*...I mean, *us*. Always will be."

"I know...I just...needed to say it. To let you know...every now and then."

He kissed her on the head again. "On a more positive note, did Sean give you my message?"

"Umm...maybe," she said, silently wondering, *I'm doubting that message was to molest my lady lumps.*

"So he rescheduled your appointment then? Since our female doctor was out...I told him to move it. Sorry for the inconvenience."

"Uhhh...well, I was booked to come back," she said, realizing her stepbrother directly disobeyed his father's order. Not wanting to get him in trouble, she wondered, *Then why did he examine me himself? He could've easily just rebooked me. Did he...want to see me naked? Is it weird that I actually...think that's hot? What's wrong with me...I need to get this out of my filthy mind. It's gross...yeah, I'll stick to that!*

"Good, Dr. Richards will be back tomorrow, so all your health needs will be fulfilled."

"Yeah...they'll definitely be filled," she said blushing, quickly escaping to her room.

*****

Time ticked by as Darcy watched the clock constantly. Lying on her bed, she studied every revolution of each hand. *When will he get here? It's late! Dad's in bed already...thankfully! How would I explain this visit to him?*

Suddenly, her bedroom door opened. Sean Abel crept in, still wearing his white medical coat.

"I didn't even hear you enter the house," she said.

"Shhh." He placed a finger to her lips. "Dad doesn't need to be woken."

She nodded in agreement. As badly as she wanted to ask why he examined her against orders, she was nervous about the answer. "OK," she whispered.

"Where's the dilator?"

"Hidden in here," she said, removing it from her side table drawer.

"Hold on to that," he ordered. The white-coated stepbrother sat beside Darcy on the bed. She was wearing a nightshirt, draped down to her knees. Her stepbrother's strong arm brushed her leg, making the redhead's thighs nervously clench. "Relax. Give control of your vagina to me...imagine me owning it," he instructed her, forcing her legs open with large bare hands. Darcy's white brief underwear showed, a wet stain upon the crotch.

With every pried inch, her nightshirt crawled further up her thighs. She pulled it down, thinking, *I know he's already seen me naked today, but there's something about my own bedroom...the house we both grew up in! It seems even badder!*

Once her legs were opened wide, stepbrother Sean forced the shirt past her asscheeks. The battle continued upward, traveling the undulating pear-shape of her hips, delving inward to her waist.

Giving up the fight, Darcy's body went limp, feeling her stepbrother grasp the panty bands. Slowly yanking, Dr. Abel slid them down his stepsister's smooth legs. Removing them through the feet, he quietly snuck them into his jacket pocket.

Why would he do that? She wondered silently. However, her mind was quickly distracted by a tube of lubricant. Sean soaked his finger.

He spread her moist red lips, instructing, "I didn't bring gloves...I'll have to use my bare hands," he announced.

"It's OK," she said, feeling a sudden urge for his touch. It was unexpected, but sexually desperate.

Massaging her velvet entrance intimately, he felt his stepsister's body shutter from mere contact. There was a vast difference between *his* touch and *her* own. "Take slow breaths for me. In and out."

She obeyed, breathing deeply. Her chest heaved up and down, further showcasing braless breasts. Nipples protruded through the bunched nightshirt. Still holding the rubber dilator, it was quickly stolen from her hand.

Dr. Sean Abel took the invader, lubing the rounded tip. Taking hold of Darcy's left hand, he led her fingers to her clit. "Remember what we did in the office. Pinch the swollen button, rub in soft circles. Draw your attention away from insertion."

Keeping his hand upon hers, the two rubbed her clit in unison. The sensation was immediate and pleasurable. Dr. Abel waited for a while, letting his stepsister patient sink into a lull of lust. Just when her body relaxed, he placed the dilator in her right hand. As it kissed her luscious lips, Darcy tightened up again.

He guided her hand, gliding the dilator into the soaked slit. Pausing at her honey pot, he said, "You have nothing to fear. I'm here with you...will protect you from pain. Together...let's penetrate you."

His words turned Darcy on to no end. Not only did her apprehension melt, she welcomed the invasion. Her bedroom setting was no longer a point of discomfort, but arousal. The most shocking fact of all? The stepbrother title was no longer a point of disgust, but newly discovered taboo desire.

Their hands intertwined, jointly gripping the dilator. Together they slid the gooey phallus inside her heavenly haven. Although Darcy's face tensed, it was more pleasure than pain. Each inch slowly disappeared into the curvy redhead. Before they knew it, all six inches were buried inside her tender tunnel. The rounded base stopped her vagina from fully swallowing it.

Before Sean Abel could lead her hand, his stepsister began slowly pumping herself. Together, their hands glided back and forth, fucking her sweet pussy. All the while, their joint touch rubbed Darcy's throbbing clit.

The redhead kept her eyes connected to her stepbrother, fixated on his stare. Letting his image stain her brain, the surrealness seemed to fuel her lust, inviting it opposed to rejecting. Although she was still spooked by its forbidden nature, the moment overrode all sense of societal guilt.

Dr. Abel's cock was rock hard. He wanted to yank the dilator out, replacing it with his manly member. Seeing her face tense, bottom lip bitten, he knew she was nearing orgasm. *This is it!* He told himself. *I'm really going to make my stepsister cum. I can even fuck her...she wants it. I...don't think I can do this! It's my stepsister! I'm a doctor. Stop it now!*

As the dilator fully entered Darcy's snatch, he removed both hands. He shut her legs. "It'll stay in...just tighten while upright. Return to my office in two days," he said, standing up and heading toward the door.

"That's it? You're just...leaving me like this?"

"Leaving you like what? I came to help you insert the dilator...I did that. Did you want something else?" he asked, interested in her response.

"Uhh, *no,*" she said, yanking the shirt back down to her knees. "See you then."

The disappointed doctor nodded, exiting the bedroom. Right as he shut the door, he exhaled, suddenly cursing his conscience. *I'm a dick! Fuck ethics! I could've nailed my sexy stepsister! Now...another chance may never come!* Exhaling in frustration, he grasped his aching sinuses. A sweet surprise suddenly hit his nose. His hand had been baptized in her holy waters.

Remembering her stolen panties, he removed them from his pocket. Placing them to his face, he inhaled deeply. Engulfed by fumes of feminine fragrance, he smothered himself in her wet crotch. Opening his mouth, he sucked upon it, wringing whatever juices he could squeeze.

If possible, he would let his breath empty for one last sniff of satisfaction. However, his moment of bliss was interrupted. "Sean?" a voice asked from the hallway.

Oh shit! Tell me that's not my father, Sean silently hoped, slowly turning his head toward the voice. Seeing Dr. Tim Abel, he wondered, *How the hell will I explain this one?* Dad!" he said, quickly removing the panties from his nose. "Sorry I didn't call first..."

"That's not a problem...you know you're always welcome home. Though, your stepsister's underwear on your face...that just *might* be a problem. Why would you do such a thing?"

Sean paused in thought. Suddenly it came to him. "It's Darcy...she needed a medical opinion."

"Is she OK?" Tim Abel asked in concern.

"I'd tell you...but...doctor-patient confidentiality...you understand."

"As the ranking doctor of the practice and *this* household...tell me now. I must say...in all my years of medicine, I've yet to see this *interesting* method."

Sean exhaled. "She just...had a question about her odor. Wanted to know if she...smelled normal. You know kids."

"Apparently I don't know kids...especially my own," he declared. "So does she...smell normal?"

"Perfect...I mean, perfectly normal," he said.

"I'm a doctor, why didn't she ask me?"

"Well, come on...you *are* her step-dad."

"And you're her stepbrother."

"Yeah, but lets be honest, that's *way* less embarrassing on the humiliation scale. Look, everything's fine. I have to get going, busy day tomorrow."

"Me too," Tim Abel said. "Spring hay fever always brings them in."

"I'll have to come back for dinner sometime, the three of us," Sean said. "Like the old days."

"Right," he agreed, still unsure about his son's questionable act.

"See you at work," Sean said, attempting to exit with panties in-hand.

"You can leave those here," Tim ordered, holding out his palm. "I'm sure your stepsister would like them returned."

Hiding his disappointment, Sean turned to his father. Handing the white wet panties to the senior doctor, he could barely let them go. Tim Abel forced them away, rubber-banding them into his own face. Darcy's scent momentarily teased his nostrils.

"Goodnight, dad," Sean said, escaping toward the front door.

Holding the panties, Tim waited for his son to leave the house. As the door shut, he examined the underwear, checking for signs of discharge or abnormality. Feeling the crotch, he felt her wetness. *Does she smell anything like her mother did? What I'd give to taste that amazing woman again,* he thought. He quickly chastised himself. *That is sick, Dr. Abel! She's your stepdaughter...not your wife!*

Setting the panties at Darcy's door, Tim returned to his master bedroom. Five quiet minutes expired before he returned. *She had a medical question...and I'm the head doctor. I better check her scent myself...for matters of Darcy's health, of course.*

He picked up the white briefs, placing the crotch to his nose. Inhaling deeply, a field of spring flowers grew inside his nostrils. An endorphin rush filled Tim Abel's body, stimulating senses that hadn't been awakened in years. Just like his son, he was overtaken by the addicting scent. Like an addict, he inhaled every fiber.

Though unlike Sean, he discovered something quite surprising. *She smells just like her mother...but even sweeter. Damn me...I shouldn't be having these thoughts. I never looked at her in a sexual way before...I can't start now!* He quickly headed for his bedroom, locking the door behind him. However, his actions betrayed his words.

He took his stepdaughter's panties with him.

*****

Darcy Smith waddled into school, avoiding friends at all costs. Sitting in her chair during first period anatomy class, she tried to remain calm. Her mind was busy recalling the prior night's sleep attempt.

Right after stepbrother Sean left her room, she turned off the light, hoping to drift off. Instead, she felt the plastic shaft occupy her innards. The more she focused on it, the bigger it felt. She tightened her legs, making her canal even tighter. Already turned on by the step-doctor's touches, the constant stimulation made her wetter than she'd ever been.

She watched the clock, hoping to be distracted by the morning alarm. After each glance, she'd groan in frustration. Mere minutes had ticked by. At some point in the night, time appeared to be heading backward.

I feel like I'm being stretched on the inside, she thought. In reality, she was quite correct. Although thinner than the average penis, the dilator's job was to both widen and adapt her to the feeling. She didn't realize it, but with each new moment, her sexual nerves were more accepting of penetration.

Curling up in a ball, her thighs clamped down on the vaginal invader. The position put more pressure upon her G-spot. Although the gland was a mystery to her, she definitely was introduced to its feeling. Beads of sexual juice trickled down her thighs.

The night hours continued to expire slowly. Darcy managed to drift off around 3 A.M., visited by vivid sexual dreams. Her visions were from the day Sean saw her changing, though she was her present age. At the time, she remembered being humiliated, seeing him standing frozen like a deer in headlights. Though in the reflective dream world, she peered upon it with new eyes.

What once appeared to be a look of disgust, was suddenly a gaze of lust. She imagined him attacking her like a bear to prey. In her mind, she was so desirable to him, he had to have her, stepsister or not.

Knocked to the bedroom floor, she imagined calling out, "Dad, Sean is..." Darcy's mouth was covered by Sean's hand, yanking his pants down with the other. Bumping his cock-head into the sweet slit, the stepbrother forced himself into her.

Her dream moans turned from cries of stolen virginity to pleasure gasps. Even in the realm of imagination, she could feel his cock deep within. It was as if he was physically entering her. Darcy's unconscious mind mentally merged plastic and skin.

The redhead's soft voice moaned into night air, her thighs choking the dilator like stepbrother cock. As the dream-doctor rammed her, a sloshing of feminine rain splashed her thighs. A sharp pinch commanded her creamy lips. When he drew back for a second thrust, a crimson covering stained Sean's shaft.

Her dream-hymen was ruptured, still intact in real life. She could feel the mixture of pleasurable pain ruminate through her sleeping body. Craving her stepbrother's total dominance, she completely submitted to his primal desires.

The dream doctor removed his hand from her mouth, pinning her arms to the floor. His thrusts continued, cock crashed into her sopping pussy. He suddenly went still, grunting into the air. Right before his forbidden dream-cum could fill her, the buzzing alarm clock sounded. Darcy awoke disappointed. She guiltily craved Sean's seed.

Sweaty and wet, she'd peeled back the covers. A massive puddle soaked the bed mattress. She felt it with a hand, wondering,

Did I pee myself in the night? After further exploration she realized it was sticky, thick and clear, definitely not urine. Although it would remain a mystery to her, she squirted in her sleep. She was so naturally tight, the dilator stayed in.

Such an experience was easy to hide in a private bedroom, though a classroom orgasm was unthinkable. Too bad for Darcy, the more she tried not to cum, the hotter the urge got. Just her luck, the teacher was discussing the sexual process.

Rocking back and forth in her hard desk-seat, the curvy redhead tightened upon the plastic phallus. The seated-angle stimulated her drastically. Having never had a conscious orgasm, she didn't realize the growing heat was a hint of coming eruption.

The Anatomy teacher's lecture echoed through Darcy's ears. "During vaginal penetration, the nerves get activated...emulating a pleasurable effect, stimulating the sexual organs. Does anyone know what that bodily response is called?"

Her class went dead silent. Even though the classmates knew the answer, they weren't admitting it. Little did they know, they were about to get a live demonstration of one.

As Darcy leaned forward, the dilator struck her G-spot. Her full bodyweight pressed the sexual gland. A massive gasp exited her lungs, a million chills shivered up her spine. The curvy redhead's sexy snatch tingled, fluttering her brain like encircling fireflies. Losing all control of her senses, she crouched down, breasts and head slumped upon the desk's surface. When the last and most powerful spasm started, she shouted, "Fucking...*cumming*!"

The class collectively gasped, watching the curvy redhead shiver in sexual ecstasy. Her moans increased, hips swayed, ass grinding against the seat. Her teacher watched in as much shock and awe as her classmates. For a moment, the young girl appeared possessed by a force of a different world.

Darcy's face was flustered, body shaking, sweaty and exhausted. She slowly recovered, simmering down. As her senses returned, she looked around the room in horrific realization. Then she stared at her surprised teacher, waiting to be suspended.

"Not exactly the official term, Miss Smith...a rather crude one, in fact. Though, correct in an...uncouth way. The proper term is called *orgasm*. Thank you for the rather...spirited, accurate demonstration...though it really wasn't necessary."

Darcy raised her hand, realizing she couldn't risk another possible occurrence. She also was unwilling to remove the dilator from within. "Can I go to the nurse...I'm feeling kinda...hot."

＊＊＊＊＊

Sean entered a pricy restaurant, taking a nervous breath. The hostess greeted him. "Good evening, sir. Table for one?"

"No...I'm meeting someone. A blind date...not quite sure what she looks like...except for red hair."

"Ah, she's waiting for you. Right this way, sir."

Sean walked the row of tables like a death-row inmate. Although he had plenty of sex over the years, he couldn't seem to commit to a relationship. It never worked out; always some flaw or excuse ending things. He had no desire to date again, though constant thoughts of his stepsister motivated him.

At first, the thoughts of her were strictly sexual. He had no qualms with the naughtiness. Sean imagined tasting Darcy's wet lust, feeling his cock dip into her tight snatch. Visions of popped-cherries danced in his head, the curvy redhead rode his cock like a dream angel.

Though once those thoughts turned romantic, overwhelming shame arrived. Sean imagined holding hands with his stepsister, lying along the riverbank, staring up at a star-pocked sky. He craved her kiss, needing to blanket her lips with his own. Then came the scariest image of all, Darcy in a white wedding dress, cuddling her new stepbrother husband on their honeymoon night.

That's when he turned to desperation. "Time to hit the Internet!" he had proclaimed. When porn didn't wash the romance away, he headed to a dating website. *I'll just find someone to replace her, direct my loving feelings toward them instead.* Scrolling the ads, no one lit his fire. *What do I want in a woman?* He'd asked himself. *Curves. Submissive. Sexy. Red hair. Holy shit...I've just described my stepsister! What's wrong with me?*

Finally finding a profile to fit his physical needs, he said, *There's nothing wrong with dating a girl who looks like Darcy...it just can't be Darcy herself. Problem solved!*

"Sean?" the curvy redhead asked from the restaurant's table.

The resemblance is pretty close...a good start, he thought, moving in to hug her. "Great to meet you, Tonya."

"You too," she said, sitting down.

"Can I start you two with an appetizer?" the waiter asked.

The two opened the menus. Before Tonya could answer, Sean ordered, "I'll have the lobster bisque, she'll have cheese sticks."

"Cheese sticks? An...*interesting* choice," she said. *It would be...if I were a child,* she silently thought.

"Drinks?"

Sean repeated his mistake. "I'll have white wine...she'll have a cherry coke, the natural kind...made with maraschinos."

An odd look crossed Tonya's face. "Again...quite an *interesting* choice, Mr. Abel."

Why the hell did I order cheese sticks and cherry Coke? he wondered. *Oh shit, that's what Darcy always orders. She never decides...has me order for her. What the fuck's wrong with me?*

The waiter walked away. Tonya addressed Sean, "I take it...you're a bit of a control freak."

"I'm sorry, it's probably just the doctor in me...prescribing medicines and diets to patients," he said, trying to cover his error.

"I *guess* I can understand that. So, I take it you're a redhead fanatic...dare I say...fetishist?"

"Why would you say that?" Sean asked.

Tonya removed a folded paper from her pocket. "I brought your dating ad with me, so I didn't misquote a word. 'I want...no, I need a redhead. I don't want brunettes or blonds or grays...I want red. I don't want a dye job, auburn, or a Raggedy Ann wig. I want fire red...blood red...cherry red hair. Nothing, I mean absolutely nothing else will do. Please don't waste my valuable time. Did I mention...RED AND RED ONLY?'"

Sean's face was the red one. "The site must've changed it on me...I didn't write that."

"I didn't realize dating websites changed ads," Tonya said, clearly not buying it.

At that moment, Sean shifted to a different topic. "So tell me, Tonya, do you go to school?"

"I do."

"Central High School?"

"*High school*? I appreciate the complement...but I'm 27 years old. I mentioned that in my email, didn't I? Graduate school...masters degree?"

"Right, slipped my mind," he said, recalling Darcy's school name instead.

Tonya's tone turned blunt. "OK, listen. We both know these dating sites are about hooking-up anyway...I'm good with that. So, ditch the weird conversation, grab a burger, get high and go fuck. Sound good?"

"It sounds...oh, why the hell not. Let's go."

*****

The door to Sean's apartment crashed open, as the two fuck-mates spilled inside. They smelled like weed and Burger King, a rather sickly combination. Their lips smacked together, bodies ground into each other, rolling on the floor.

Tonya reached into Sean's pants, grabbing for his glory. Suddenly, she stopped. "Whoa...you're soft?"

Sean paused in horrific realization. "I am?" he asked in disbelief.

"Man, you realize you have control over these things...right?"

"Give me a minute," he said, sticking a hand in his pants to join Tonya's. Together they started masturbating flaccid cock, trying frantically to revive it. The doctor's heart rate increased, embarrassment level rose. *This has never happened before! Think of something damn it...my man card will be removed if anyone in this town hears about it! For all I know, this shit will go viral on Facebook! Trolls love drama!*

As the two-minute mark expired, Sean was desperate. He tried summoning threesomes, foursomes, spanking, choking, and extreme fantasies like bukkake. Nothing worked. On the verge of breakdown, he went to his last resort: Darcy in the gyno chair. That's when his cock roared to life.

"Hey, hey! Somebody woke up," Tonya said, leaning down to suck it.

Sean pulled away in panic and self-disgust. Forcing the dual hands from his pants, he rose in shame. Pulling his Internet date to her feet, he led her to the door. "You gotta go."

"Man...are all doctors buzz kills like you?"

"I hear pot dealers are more fun...I'm sure you'll hit it off," he said, opening the door, pushing Tonya out. Closing it, Sean slid down to the ground. Leaning his head against the door, he sighed. *It appears I'm addicted to my stepsister. I'm in deep shit.*

*****

The redheaded patient awaited her step-doctor in the gyno chair. Two days of dilation went by, multiple orgasms accompanied them. By appointment time, the feeling was starting to grow on her. *I wonder if I could leave it in permanently?* She wondered.

A knock on the door sounded, as the step-doctor entered. "Darcy," Sean Abel said with a smile and hug. "How'd it feel? It appears you survived the stuffing."

"You kinda forgot to mention the part where I'd...cum in class!" she exclaimed.

"That's not a given...though, is *that* a bad thing?"

"The cum part...*not* bad. The class thing...kinda bad."

"It's not like you can time these things. I'd assume that was your first orgasm."

She blushed. "It was...had a few since...without even touching myself. I guess that means I'm cured?"

"Not so fast, stepsister. *That* dilator was only a small step. You won't fully be cured until you've faced...a *penis*. At least something of equal value, size and girth. You don't want your first time ruined because we didn't push your limits."

"But...what about the cherry popping?"

He paused, thinking long and hard. His thoughts matched the growing cock within his pants. *As quickly as she responded to the dilator, I've got one last shot. If I let her walk away without making a move, the chance will never come again. I know it's risking everything...but the chance to fuck my stepsister is worth my entire career.* "Good point, Darcy. In fact, that's something we have to discuss."

"Should I go offer myself to the football team? That should get the job done."

"No!"

"Just kidding," she giggled.

Sean wiped his sweat-covered forehead, clearly nervous about his upcoming suggestion. "Losing your virginity is an important life moment. I don't want you just tossing it away to a random loser."

"Really? I heard the first time sucks."

"Well, with high school boys...you're likely correct."

"Boys are my only options...unless you know a man willing to de-cherry me?"

Sean's cock stiffened, his eyes fixated upon the tight juicy gap between her spread legs. The dilator was still in-place. "I happen to know a man...who'd cherish the job more than anything in the world."

"Do tell," she begged excitingly.

Doctor Sean Abel rose tall. Unbuttoning his white medical coat, the outline of his cock stared back. His confused stepsister stared at the concealed weapon in awe. Her confusion lessened as his slacks and underwear hit the floor. A thick, hard 7-inch cock pointed towards its prey.

"Holy crap! Are you saying...that man's...*you*?" she asked.

He moved toward the reclined patient, draping his body over hers. His strong chest was still covered with a button-up shirt and red tie. The white medical coat swayed behind him in an air-conditioned breeze. Darting right for his stepsister's mouth, he kissed her passionately.

Darcy's breath came to a dead stop. She froze, asking herself, *Did my stepbrother just stick his tongue in my mouth? Is this another dream? Cuz if so...I'm not sure I wanna wake up...ever.*

The deeper Sean kissed his stepsister, the harder his cock pressed against her sweet pink abyss. Finally forced to accept the moment as reality, Darcy's tongue decided to play back.

Having kissed boys before, she quickly felt the difference of a man. The 30-year-old stepbrother licked the 18-year-old's throat. The kiss was hot, nasty and passionate. The taboo nature made it even hotter.

As the doctor withdrew from her mouth, he bit her bottom lip hard. Sliding downward, he thrust the paper gown open, tearing it apart. Licking down her chin to her neck, he continued into the breasted valley. Climbing the C-cup mountains he licked each areola in-turn. His teeth gnashed nipples, causing stinging pleasurable-pain, refusing to stop until his stepsister begged him to.

He continued down her soft belly, leaving bite-marks and kisses along the trail. Finally arriving at her shaved snatch, he slid down the lips. Crossing the swollen clit, he paused to tease it with a few tongue strokes. Darcy's curvy body trembled, liquid lust dripped down her stepbrother's cheeks.

Heading downward, he arrived at her luscious love pot. He licked around the dilator's rounded outer rim, teasing his patient. With no warning, he yanked the plastic invader from within. Pleased to see her hymen fully intact, he was ready to take her virginity.

However, he couldn't deny himself more of her sweet wine. Seeing a large offering of sticky satisfaction upon the medical dildo, he stuck the shaft in his mouth. Deep throating it, he sucked every bit of his stepsister's cum from it.

Once that was cleared, he dove into her creamy spread lips. Awash in the redhead's lust, he fucked her with his spastic tongue. Darting in and out of her honey-hole, he practically took her virginity with his mouth.

Darcy's girly moans filled the air, reminding Sean that others were present outside the door. He stood, covering her mouth with his latex-gloved hand. Pressing his cock to her pussy, he rubbed the mushroom-shaped head along her silk curtains.

The moment of truth arrived. Both doctor and patient, stepbrother and sister, stared each other in the eyes. Each of them nodded. It was more than the look of silent permission; it was a gaze of desperate desire.

Keeping his hand over Darcy's mouth, he pushed inside her. The thick head was barely through before a *pop* sounded. A sharp lustful cry muffled from the redhead. Before she could confirm a hymen rupture, her stepbrother claimed her. Soft, wet, tight and silky, Sean could've cum right then. Pressed up against his stepsister's bare body, he knew she deserved a better first time than a quickie.

Forcing his own needs away, he momentarily withdrew. Sure enough, a liquid sheath of crimson evidence covered his cock. Showing proof to his stepsister, chills crossed her skin. The weight of the moment hit her. *I've just lost my virginity...to my stepbrother!*

Oh shit...this is nuts! Even crazier? I want more. "Take me, doctor," she begged.

Abandoning any thoughts of condoms, an even hotter thought crossed Sean's mind. *I'll cum inside my fertile stepsister. Oh fuck...this keeps getting more wrong...and right at the same fucking time.*

Dipping back into his spread patient, her popped cherry lubricated him more. Five inches were swallowed immediately, though two more waited their turn. He drove forward hard and unapologetically. Bumping her cervical wall, his cock forced her to adapt to him.

Darcy's legs tensed in the stirrups, stretched by both length and girth. There were so many sensations and shocks, the Vaginismus pain was long abandoned. Her mind was too busy focusing on the hot stepbrother pounding her juicy pussy.

Refusing to quit, Dr. Sean Abel drove deeper into Darcy. His cock gained new ground with each landing. Before he knew it, all 7-inches disappeared inside the red sea. He grasped her breasts, pulling her into him by the nipples. Her thick ass slid back and forth across the slick gyno chair.

Dr. Abel fucked his stepsister so hard strands of red hair flew like Medusa's serpent locks. Each thrust stretched Darcy more, her canal remade. There was no question, the virgin was headed toward orgasm.

She felt physical and emotional heights never imagined in her 18-years. Suddenly, a new aid added to her excitement: stepbrother sperm. A thick load of Sean's cum squirted into the young girl.

White streams exploded into her fertile body, seeping toward her womb.

The heavy stepbrother seed pushed Darcy over the edge. Screaming inside Sean's hand-gag, she bit down on his finger. He grunted, feeling both the pain of teeth and boiling spurts of semen released.

Darcy's body shook like the possessed, trembling in waves of static pleasure. A million sparks lit her brain, chills popped from her every pore. Her eyes stayed open the entire time. As her womb soaked in sperm, her mind absorbed the sexy stepbrother, mentally taping the taboo scene. Darcy's last spasm timed perfectly to Dr. Abel's final load.

Collapsing on his patient, he rested his head on her breasts. Staying inside her until flaccid, the two of them remained silent. Together, they simultaneously thought the same thing.

What the fuck did we just do? Will we talk about it later? Never mention it? A one-time thing? Multi hookup thing? Could this really turn into a...relationship? As if hearing each other's thoughts, they both gazed at each other. Neither of them had an answer to unspoken questions.

*****

After awkwardly cleaning up and getting dressed, the two snuck from the room. They hoped no one heard their moans, though that worry suddenly took on new life.

"Dad!" Sean said.

"Step-dad!" Darcy followed in an equally horrified tone.

He paused in surprise, realizing they exited the same exam room. "What were you both up to in there? You weren't examining your sister...were you?"

A long pause followed. Sean Abel thought, *Dad will check the patient records, see she was my patient. I can't hide it. Shit!* "That's a long story...not sure Darcy wants her health issues shared *here*," he said.

"Right," she agreed.

The senior doctor had made it clear: his stepdaughter was to be examined by the female doctor only. Already suspicious of, *the panty-smelling visit*, Dr. Tim Abel was about to call their bluff. "Then come to dinner...tomorrow night. You can tell me there. It'll be just the three of us...family only. Like the old days."

Both Darcy and Sean turned pale. Only they knew that one major difference existed from days of old.

The stepbrother and stepsister had sex.

CHAPTER THREE

After the appointment, Darcy drove straight home. In a near daze, she aimlessly walked the confines of her bedroom. Zombie-like in nature, she wondered how she got from stepbrother disgust to lust in a matter of days. Though in reality, her attraction to him always lingered beneath the surface. The greater it got, the more she had convinced herself of the opposite.

The past no longer mattered as the deed was done. Their future was unknown. She was sore in a good way, though the constant reminder was not so good. *Can I really just go on like it never happened?* She wondered. *What if he never brings it up again? It will be so weird around him! Will it kill our relationship...or could it make it stronger? Uh...I wish he'd just appear!*

Granting her wish, Sean opened Darcy's bedroom door. "Do you mind if I come in?" he asked.

After a startled gasp, she paused, looking upon him with new eyes. The older brother suddenly gave her butterflies, making her heart race. She was speechless. "Sean...uh, yeah, uh...come in."

He entered, also void of words. Both kept a fair distance, looking away in awkwardness. "I guess we should...at least discuss it. Unless...you'd rather just pretend it never happened..."

"No!" she shouted, realizing how desperate she sounded. "I wanna talk about it...just...don't know what to say."

"Then that makes two of us. I honestly didn't plan any of this...it just happened."

"Me either," she said. "But can I ask you something?"

"Anything."

"Do you...regret it? Was it just a...mistake to you?"

"No!" he said with conviction. "You could never be my mistake. I'm...*honored* to be the man who took your virginity."

"Really?" she said with a bright smile.

"Truly. I just hope...you don't regret losing it to your stepbrother."

"If you'd asked me before you took it...I'd swear I would've regretted it. Though, if I had to do it over again...you'd be the one and only," she said sincerely.

A flattered look crossed Sean's face. "Thank you. I hope you still think that way...while lying to your friends about the guy who deflowered you."

She paused in deep thought, "I never really thought about that. Do I have to?"

"Lie? No...but would you really want *that* to get out? The stepbrother thing might not be so accepted."

"True...rumor central."

"You bet. The talk of the school...maybe town as well."

"But really...is it so bad? It's not like we're born from the same parents. I mean...it's not like we'll have a three-headed kid or anything."

"No, it's not unlawful or even wrong...but you know how cruel people can be."

"Will you tell...friends?"

Now Sean was the one to pause, unsure if he'd let the secret out. "Hmmm...would you want to be my bragging right?"

"Maybe," she said bashfully.

"I'd be proud to brag about you," he said boldly.

She smiled, feeling special. "Would you tell...dad?"

"No!" he said emphatically. "And neither would you."

"So you're not *that* proud, I guess."

"He'd lose his mind!"

She mentally imagined the consequences. "OK...I see your point. He'd kinda freak out."

"He didn't even want me examining you...as a *doctor*. If I told him we're fuck buddies...he'd castrate me."

"So is that all we are...fuck buddies? I mean...I won't be mad if it is...I guess I just felt something else inside."

"What did you feel?"

Darcy blushed, "You first."

Sean Abel shifted from his head, examining his heart. "I don't know how to define us...but I know it's more than just sex."

A sigh of relief exited Darcy's mouth. "Like how much more...exactly?"

Not knowing what to say, he stretched his hands out a distant length. "*That* much?"

"Come on...seriously, Sean."

"I don't know yet...I've not had enough time to think it over. It's all so new...unexpected. I just know...I want more."

"So is it like...love?"

"Whoa...step-sis...that's taking things a bit fast."

"Sorry, I've read too many erotic romance eBooks."

"I'm not saying no...to love."

"Really?"

"Definitely not. Though I'm not saying yes either...it's too soon. Love's more than a few orgasms, you know?"

"The truth is...I *don't* know. I guess I just wanna know where that leaves us. We're not just step-sex-siblings...and we're not in love? So what *are* we?"

"If we must have a title...let's call it...seeing each other?"

"Is that a boyfriend-girlfriend thing?"

Apprehension painted Sean's face. He knew agreeing could be jumping the gun on his commitment level. However, he didn't want to upset her. "Sure."

A rush of emotion flooded Darcy's young heart. She hadn't even been with a serious boyfriend yet. "Wow! You'd be my first official one."

"Just remember...we're keeping it loose for now. At least until we...figure out our future plans."

"Our *future*," Darcy said in newfound youthful bliss. "That sounds so weird...but so cool. Would we hide it from people...like family? Do I tell friends?"

"Bottom line...if someone doesn't ask...we won't tell," he winked.

A smile crossed Darcy's lips. The fear, which plagued her, suddenly lifted. "Fair enough. I can't believe we're gonna do this! Are you sure you want this?" she asked. "I don't wanna hurt your reputation with the family. I also don't want my heart broken."

"You're worth *that* risk."

"Is it weird...I feel like I've always belonged to you? Well, like I've always belonged to you and step-dad. And it's not like I'd date him," she said with a giggle.

A disturbed look crossed Sean's face. Ignoring her words, he stepped up to her, held her chin, and claimed her full lips for himself. Although they'd kissed in the exam room, the current act was much more powerful. It bared more importance than before. Although it was still a stepbrother kissing his forbidden stepsister, it was now a man kissing his girl.

*****

"Pass the potatoes, please," the salt and pepper haired, Tim Abel asked his son. Sean passed the dish, careful not to make eye contact with his father. Darcy picked at her food, remaining quiet as well. "Not quite like the old days, I guess." Tim sadly sighed. He could still see his deceased wife sitting beside him, her chair reserved, place still set. "Can't blame a man for trying. I even tried cooking her food...though, who am I kidding?"

"I think it tastes great, step-dad," Darcy said with a warm smile. "Just like mom used to make it."

He returned the smile, thankful for the kind support. "Thanks, Darcy. I can always count on you to lift my spirits."

Sean grimaced, appearing to be sickened by his father's words.

Tim Abel continued. "I haven't asked in a while...how's school going?"

"Fine," she said, lowering her head again. It was clear she feared spilling the relationship beans. As nervous as she was, it was bound to be blurted.

"Are you feeling better?"

"Much," she answered, wanting to keep any health questions as short as possible. She remembered the real reason for their gathering.

Tim turned his eyes toward his son. "How's your side of the practice going?"

"Fine," Sean said, keeping his head down like his sister. He took a drink of water.

"Satisfied patients?"

Sean choked on the water, unable to erase the image of a sexually satisfied stepsister. "Very," he sparingly offered.

Unimpressed by the lack of conversation, Tim Abel moved onto the night's main event. "Well, since we're obviously not in a small talk mood...let's address that long story...you didn't have time for, doctor."

Sean kept eating, pretending he wasn't being addressed. After a long pause, he looked up, stared down by his father and stepsister. "Me?"

"No...your doctor-sister. Of course, *you*."

"I don't think Darcy wants her issues discussed over meatloaf."

"I saw her records. I know why she was there. My question was...what were you both doing in the same exam room? Did you examine your own sister?"

"Dad...please! Do you really think...I'd examine my *sister*?"

"Well?"

"No, I would *not*! It's insulting and preposterous! Now...examining my *non*-blood relation *stepsister*...is a different story."

"You didn't!"

"Dad, I just wanted to offer a perspective...a female doctor couldn't. It was harmless, right Darcy?"

"Right."

"I'll be the judge of that," Tim Abel said. "And besides, I strictly forbid family examinations. You know that includes extended and step family. Darcy's your sister. Examining her body is no different than dating her...something you'd never do." Both of them looked down in embarrassment, blushing. The senior doctor picked up the awkwardness. "Or would you?"

"What do you think? Never!" Sean shouted.

"Well...a gyno exam is like getting to third base. You're one at bat away from a grand-slam...if you catch my drift."

Again both Darcy and Sean gazed downward in awkward embarrassment.

Tim Abel's face lit up with sick shock. "Oh no...don't say you did that too!"

"I didn't say anything of the sort," Sean said.

"Your expression said it all! The underwear suddenly makes sense."

Darcy squinted in confusion. "Underwear? I don't get it?"

An enraged Sean shouted, "Bullshit! I'm a professional...you have no right to accuse me of such lies! And speaking of expressions...the look on your face is jealousy. You're just mad you didn't get her in *your* gyno chair!"

Darcy gasped, staring up at her stepfather. She silently wondered, *Jealous? Why would he be jealous of his son examining me? Mad or sickened...I'd get...but jealous? Could he have feelings for me too? No way.*

Tim Abel retorted, "How dare you insinuate that about my stepdaughter! You're the sick one here, not me! And you should be damn grateful I made you a partner right out of med school! Just so you know...that can easily be undone."

"Then undo it! But I won't sit back and let you trash my name!"

Darcy's eyes watered, seeing her stepbrother and father get more heated. The two men leaned further over the table, fingers poking each other's chests. Soon, their fists were clenched, nearing signs of a physical fight. The redhead panicked in silent confusion. *I have to stop this...I can't let them kill each other. I'll take the blame.* "We're dating!" she shouted. "It's my fault...I made him have doctor sex with me!"

Both Sean and Tim paused their argument, turning their gazes toward Darcy. "What?" they shouted in unison.

"We're a couple now, well...kinda."

"Darcy!" Sean shouted in sickness. "We agreed to keep it private."

"You were both gonna kill each other. I had to stop it."

"This breaks my heart," Tim Abel said, standing up at the dinner table. "My own son and daughter...shaming the family."

Sean shouted, "She's your Stepdaughter! And you're the one who should be ashamed. Comparing every woman you date to *her*."

"I loved your step-mother very much. Moving on takes time. It's natural to compare a loved one..."

"I wasn't talking about my step-*mother*. I'm talking about...my stepsister."

Darcy gasped deeply. "Huh?"

"You have no idea what you're talking about, son!" the father shouted. "It's not true...tell her it's not, right now or..."

"Or what? You'll disown me as a son? I got news for you...that's been going on for years. I'm tired of being forgotten...getting in the way of your obsession. You even gave me the job...out of pure guilt.

"You were practically an adult when Darcy lost her mother. You were capable of taking care of yourself...she was *not*! This is a complete farce, son! Tell her *that*...now!"

"It's true, all of it...Darcy!"

"You're a damn liar!"

"Everyone you dated had to have red hair...never red enough. They weren't good enough mothers to her. You were too busy taking her to the movies or dinner...canceling your dates...ending your relationships! After mom's death, you took her pics down...Darcy's went up in her place. Mine were nowhere to be found."

"Get out!"

"Fine...though know this. Darcy has another appointment booked with me tomorrow. She's keeping it...and so am I," he said, heading for the exit.

"Sean...wait!" Darcy shouted, chasing her stepbrother out the door.

"Shit!" Tim cursed, banging a fist on the dining room table. Heading to his master bedroom, he fumed in fury. As disturbed as he was about the relationship, his son's accusations angered him more. Though as much as lies stung the senior doctor, exposed truths were like daggers to his soul.

Turning towards family photos on the wall, the evidence confronted him. Tim Abel was guilty. Each picture featured his stepdaughter's beautiful face. He was in some of them, though Sean was absent from all. Each image was from after his wife's death, not one from before.

Grasping his salt and pepper hair, he yanked on it in frustrated self-doubt. He'd always seen himself as a proud father, though for the first time, he wondered, *Was it more than that? Was it lust? As the years went by...could a protective parental love have grown into something more? Was I mentally awaiting her to turn 18, living in denial? It can't be. Sean...can't be right!*

Moving into his closet, he unveiled every photo album. The books with his deceased wife were buried at the bottom, hidden from his pained heart. His son's pictures were barely above that. Up at the pile's top, in separate plastic boxes, were Darcy's photos.

Flipping through each page, photos of his stepdaughter and himself appeared. No one else was in them. The senior doctor kept assuring himself, "No...no, it's just a coincidence. There have to be some of me and my son."

However, new pages turned into new books. Tossing each one aside, the desperate man was faced with a virtual mirror of his heart. He had no recollection of grouping all their photos, though he remembered little from those days anyway. It wasn't alcohol he turned to, but denial. *Doctors don't break, they stay strong for everyone else,* he remembered thinking.

An instant loss of his wife was surreal to him. Mrs. Abel was the air he breathed, reason to rise each morning. She showed him unconditional love like no other. Preparing breakfast, lunch and dinner, she made sure the doctor was always presentable, along with the kids. Each of them was kissed before the day's start and end. The couple's sex life was as passionate and warm as a winter's fire.

She was the family's glue, keeping them together. Such a loss was so traumatic to the unit, Tim went into shock of the heart. On the outside, the man appeared to be unbreakable, steel-plated. Having to be strong for Darcy, he retired all emotion of his own. Taking on the role of an every-parent, he saved his hurting stepdaughter with an over-abundance of love. Unfortunately, nothing remained for his older son. Unconsciously pushed aside, Sean was never his father's top priority again.

As everything rushed backed to his memory, Tim Abel's walls only grew taller. All defenses went into overdrive. He began throwing the books around, smashing them into walls. "I don't look at her like that!" he shouted. "I...can't! I'm...her stepfather!"

All hell broke loose. Rushing to the pictures on the walls, he tossed each one to the wood floor. Glass shattered with each landing. Every image of Darcy was torn up as if ripped from his conscious.

When that didn't remove his shame, he ran to family photo books. Carrying box after box, he dumped them all into a dry bathtub. Seeing Darcy's cotton-brief panties on his bedroom floor, he picked them up too. They were tossed in the tub.

Grabbing a bottle of rubbing alcohol, he poured liquid streams over the books. Lighting a match, he tossed it into the porcelain oval. A burst of flames leapt upward, nearly burning the senior doctor Abel. Barely escaping searing heat, he leapt up on the tub's unlit edge. Raising his hands to the heated air, he shouted, "Die damn it! Burn the pain away...burn!" He sounded like a madman.

Though even as photographic memories melted, Tim Abel's guilt wasn't cleansed. It hurt deeper than ever. Leaning inward to the fire, he wondered, *Maybe I must be cleansed instead?* Inches from descending into a tub of fire, he leapt backward. Turning on the shower, the flames slowly died off.

Quickly hurrying into the kitchen, he frantically searched through his liquor cabinet. The man didn't drink, though got them as gifts and decor pieces. Reaching for the oldest date he could find, he opened a bottle of Russian Vodka. Dumping it down his throat, the first drops of liquid fire spilled downward.

Spitting the sea of spirits from his mouth, the doctor in him shouted, "Pure poison. What the hell is wrong with people drinking this fermented death! Health hazard!"

Dumping the bottle down the sink, he looked over at a full rack of knives. Then he stared down at his wrists. Dark thoughts sailed his head. *Slitting a wrist is just a cry for help...takes hours to die. No...the neck...carotid artery is the way to do it...quick and resolute.* Removing a sharp butcher knife, he looked at his reflection in the gleaming silver. Pausing moment of sanity, he came to a conflicted confusion. *I can't live with loving her. I'm not sure I can live...without her love,* he shamefully admitted. *I can only choose one.*

His usually doctor-steady hand trembled. Placing the sharp blade to his throat area, he slowly pressed inward. Feeling the sharp sting stimulate his skin, a million thoughts raced his mind. His life flashed before him as the cliché suggests. However, within those thoughts, clarity formed.

Dropping the knife to the granite countertop, the desperate man thought, *If I can just make love to her...like I once did my wife...the pain will finally stop. Years of suffering will end. I choose to live...to love her...to save myself...no matter what it takes. Even if it costs me my son.*

Tim fled to Darcy's bedroom, inhaling upon entrance. Like an aggressive dog in heat, he could practically smell her fresh teen pussy. Heading for her dirty clothes hamper, he buried his face inside it. Breathing deeply, he dug deeper for worn undergarments.

He trembled in newfound addiction, craving her scent like a crack head seeking snort. Frantically needing to cum, he lifted the hamper, heading to the bed. Dumping the contents on silk sheets, Darcy's jeans, skirts, blouses, bras, and many panties rained down. Like an Olympic diver, he dove into the pile, drowning in worn laundry.

Rolling around in feminine clothes, he lowered his pants. Darcy's stepfather placed panties over his head and cock. He stroked himself hard. Each used undergarment was stained with newly wet lust.

The intensity was immediate. Not only had he foregone orgasm for ages, the man was driven to sexual bliss. It was one he'd only felt with Darcy's mother. With every sniff and stroke he imagined himself fucking his stepdaughter in her bed. It felt so real, he could've sworn she was riding him. He squeezed his 8-inch cock, emulating her tightness clamping his manhood.

In just moments, the overwhelming sensation brought him to eruption. One squirt soaked the panties. Each following stream escaped the underwear, creaming his stomach, Darcy's clothes and bed sheets.

As the amazing sensation ended, Dr. Tim Abel relaxed in his stepdaughter's bed. He grasped her clothes in her arms, like he was holding her tightly. It was just like he'd held her mother, with all the love and care in the world.

Tim made up his mind. *I'll take my stepdaughter away from my son. No matter what I must do to get her...I must get my life back again.*

*****

Darcy followed Sean home, driving closely behind him. Tears rolled down her cheeks, knowing she had caused him to flee. *Why didn't I keep my dumb mouth shut? I spoke out of fear...thought it would stop their yelling. I can't lose Sean...I need him,* she thought, suddenly pausing in newfound self-discovery. *What am I thinking? How can I feel so strongly already? One minute I was sickened by the thought of loving him...now I can't live without him? I don't understand these feelings...it's like...they'd always been there. Could I have just hidden them all this time?*

Arriving at her stepbrother's house, she chased him to the front door, begging, "Sean, please don't be mad at me. I'm sorry."

He unlocked his door, stopping before opening it. Slowly turning around, he said, "Look, step-sis, I'm not sure this is going to work."

"You're dumping me? Already?"

"It's not dumping...just...pausing the relationship part. You weren't supposed to tell dad about us! What the hell were you thinking?"

"You two were gonna kill each other! I had to do something. Besides, you said you weren't ashamed of me."

"I'm not! I can handle friends...maybe extended family...but Dad?"

"I'm sorry for following you home...I'm not trying to be all...stalkerish. But, you said something at dinner. I have to know..."

"It was true," Sean said, looking down in regret.

Darcy looked shocked, flattered and nauseous all in one expression. "You really think step-dad...*wants* me...like in a...horny way?"

After a long pause, Sean forced the words from his mouth. "I shouldn't have made that accusation...it wasn't my place."

"But you did, Sean...so you have to tell me...please! I can't believe it's true...he's my...stepfather! Him wanting to screw me is...weird."

"You mean like...banging your stepbrother type of weird?"

"Not the same...exactly," she said.

"You'll have to explain *that* one."

"Uhh, hello? He's ancient...like in his 50's. You're not near as old."

"What does that have to do with love? Some people would have issues with an 18-year-old dating a 30-year-old."

"Ok, if you need another reason...he had sex with my mother! Just the thought of his hands touching me...lips kissing me...penis entering me..." she paused, suddenly feeling her nipples launch from their pink pads. A rich moistness percolated between her thighs. The thought of her sexual stepfather unintentionally excited her. Vulnerable and embarrassed, she quickly overstressed the words. "It'll NEVER happen...ever!"

"Just forget I said it. You should get home. He's probably worried about you. The truth is...I'm also worried about him...he looked a bit nuts."

"So I should be the one to get axe murdered?"

"He wouldn't hurt you...you know that. He calls you his red rose."

Darcy tried to forget Tim's vast use of the pet name. It was always cute to her, though suddenly had a much different connotation. "I need to know where we stand. Sean, I know I tried to act cool earlier...pretend I didn't care. But I do care. Can we please try to continue?"

Sean felt the same deep feelings in his heart. However, logic and fear was beginning to override emotion. He imagined wrecking his family unit, destroying his career, and breaking Darcy's young heart in the process. "I care too. I just...think we need to slow things down."

"So no more sex?"

"I never said that."

"So we're just a hookup after all?"

"Let's just call us undefined...in exploration mode. In fact, if someone comes along...your age...date them. I don't want you losing the best sexual years of your life...just for me."

A deep pain pierced Darcy's chest. She got to experience heartbreak before officially knowing love. She sadly thought, *But I don't want anyone else. I want you!* However her young pride spoke instead. "There's this boy in my math class, I think he likes me," she said, trying to make him jealous.

The sickened look upon Sean's face indicated her success. "And I'll stay busy as well," he declared, trying not to look out sexed by a high-school student.

I feel like I'm gonna vomit, she thought. *Relax, maybe he just means busy as in...extra guy butt exams.* "Good," she said, trying hard to seem like she didn't care.

"So we're still on for tomorrow's appointment? That is...if you're not busy with...math homework?" Sean said jealously.

"I think I can put down the algebra book for *a bit*. But what if stepfather sees us? He was serious...deadly serious. I mean, he's also your boss."

"Then he can physically stop me. Too bad for him...it'll happen during his lunch break," he said, winking at her.

A nervous breath exited Darcy's lungs. "If you say so, Sean. I hope it doesn't backfire on us."

"You're in good hands." He hugged Darcy, gently kissing her forehead.

Uh, it's like I'm being kissed goodnight by my stepfather! Actually, forget that. Knowing what I know now...he'd probably kiss me more sexually. What a crazy night!

Pressed against his sexy stepsister, Sean's hormones took over. After a long pause, he tilted Darcy's face toward his. Leaning inward, he engulfed her lips. All Darcy's disappointment melted away, as a single kiss revealed Sean's hidden truth. His doubtful words were disproven by passion.

Afterward, the two gazed at each other. *Now that was no step-family kiss,* Darcy thought, dizzy with erotic buzz.

"Get home...I don't want dad calling out the National Guard. I know him...he won't mention tonight's drama to you...too embarrassed to admit it. It'll all blow over by morning."

"What happens after I'm cured? Does it all end?"

"Let's take one exam at a time, OK step-sis?" he said with a smile.

"I can do that," she said untruthfully.

"Just know, even if this never goes beyond sex, nothing changes between us. We'll always be close," he said, hugging her tightly.

"Nope...nothing changes," she agreed, hiding within Sean's strong arms. Conflict tore her in two. Her stepbrother's touch melted her heart, his words poisoned it. She couldn't imagine him loving someone else. Unfortunately, it was likely to be in his future. They were no longer boyfriend and girlfriend, but undefined fuck buddies. Darcy knew such a breakup would destroy their bond, though tried to believe her own lies. Sighing quietly, she tried to hide it.

Every moment Darcy hugged Sean, her warmth seeped into his soul. Burying his nose into her hair, the smell of passion fruit entered his nostrils. *I can't believe I told her to see others!* He thought. *What if she falls in love? What if I lose her? I know it would probably be in her best interest...though, can I really live with giving her up?* He gasped, realizing his own uncomfortable truth. *Could I be in love with her? Is that why I can't settle with another woman? Why I can't get her off my mind? I blamed my father for his obsession...what if I'm the one obsessed?*

"Sean, can I ask you one more question?"

"Sure."

"What happens if dad makes you choose?"

"Between what?"

"Me...or the job?"

He remained quiet. "Then I'll have one tough choice to make. Honestly...I don't know the answer. I worked so hard to get here..."

Sadness filled Darcy's heart, as she wished he'd chosen her. However, she knew it wasn't a fair question to ask. Breaking the hug, Darcy said, "I'd want you to follow your heart. No matter what you choose. Sleep well, stepbrother." Her voice was low, sadness tainted her tone. She headed toward her car.

"If I followed my heart...I'd choose you," he said aloud. Unfortunately for Sean, it didn't escape his lips until Darcy had driven away.

*****

Darcy snuck into her house, quietly shutting the door. The lights were low as she searched for her stepfather. She was happy he'd gone to bed. Entering the kitchen, she grabbed a water from the fridge.

Looking at the counter, she noticed an empty bottle of vodka. *He doesn't drink alcohol,* she thought. Next to that, a sharp-bladed kitchen knife lay purposeless, removed from its holder. Darcy gasped in nervousness. *OMG!* The man's earlier angry outburst echoed through her mind, as worst case scenarios played inside her head.

Trying to stay quiet, she hurried toward his bedroom. Inching the door open, she saw his outline in the bed sheets. He turned over, as she exhaled in relief. Quietly shutting the door, the last thing she needed was confrontation. Relieved her stepfather didn't self-harm, Darcy headed into her bedroom.

Exhausted and confused, she removed her clothes and climbed into bed. Dropping her head onto the pillow, she hoped to drift quickly into dreamland. To her shock, a lotion-like sensation soothed from beneath.

She quickly turned on the light. After a close study, she said, "No way! Could this really be...*sperm* on my sheets?" It was still puddled, a pearly shade of white. She dipped her finger in it, bringing it to her nose. Sniffing it, Darcy wondered, *How's that gonna help me? Am I some type of sperm sniffing search dog?*

Looking over at her opened hamper closet, she remembered, *I always keep that closed.* Gazing downward, a trail of panties led the way forward. It suddenly hit her. *Holy shit...Sean was telling the truth. My stepfather...wants me! In fact...he came in my bed!*

Staring back down at the cum on her finger, a primal urge overcame her. *I've never tasted cum before.* Without another thought, she stuck the fingertip in her mouth, sucking the man-frosting. Letting it slide around her tongue, each taste bud was awakened to a new experience. Savory, yet sweet, it slid down her slippery throat. After a few moments of pause, she craved more.

Licking her bed sheets, she drank as much of the taboo tonic as possible. Right as she ingested the last drop, a voice sounded from the door. "Are you moving in with him?"

The startled girl gasped in embarrassment. Wiping her mouth of white evidence, she said "Step-dad! I thought you were asleep? What do you mean? Move in with who?"

"With your stepbrother. Since you're...an *item* now," he said, a sick look upon his face.

"It's not like that...we're not even really together."

"So you lied to me?"

"Not really."

"So you *are* together then?"

"Not really either."

"I raised you better than this? You were always open and honest with me."

"I was being honest...it's just...complicated."

"Then tell me, Darcy. Are you and Sean in a relationship...or aren't you?"

"No...but kinda."

Frustration filled Tim, as he moved in towards her. Darcy froze in fear. "What are you doing, step-dad?"

Tim Abel lifted her from the bed, bra and panties masking Darcy's body. He placed her over his knees, ass up. He responded, "I'm punishing you. You wanna act like a little girl...I'll treat you like one."

"Are you really gonna...spank me, step-dad? Aren't I too old for that?"

"As long as you're under my roof...you're never to old for discipline. With what I've learned tonight...I clearly didn't spank you or your brother *enough*."

He lowered his stepdaughter's panties to her ankles. The white briefs slipped off one foot, hanging loosely on the opposite. Tim's palm stiffened, so did his cock. Adding to Darcy's shock, she felt her stepfather's manly member grow beneath her. She wondered if it was another erotic dream, though a loud snap proved its reality.

As the stepfather's hand landed upon butt-cheeks, Darcy squirmed on the older man's lap. The feeling of her thick pussy lips made him harder. His hand rose higher into the air, crashing down upon feminine curves. *Crackle!*

One pop away from a Rice Krispie, her tense body awaited the next spanking. Her mind drifted to childhood, remembering spankings from the past. Though, there was something about the man's delivery, which differed presently. Back then it was clearly a lesson, nothing sexual. The current act was arousing for them both, even if they wished it wasn't.

Another *smack* crossed her sweet buns, stinging them sharply. Each landing got harder, leaving a larger red print in its wake. Foreign chills and sensations crossed Darcy's skin, tingling her tiger-box. Her head dangled in air, bra-covered breasts swayed in rocking rhythm. The position engorged them more, nipples strained to be freed from their cloth prison.

"You'll tell me the truth!" an angered Tim Abel shouted, unleashing more stepdaughter spankings. Redness soon covered the pear-shaped porcelain canvass. Her clit rubbed against Tim's hardened, clothed cock.

After a few more spanks, something unexpected happened. The curvy redhead moaned, squirming uncontrollably upon her stepfather's lap. Tim paused in shock, seeing his stepdaughter writhe in forbidden pleasure. Waves of taboo lust sailed through Darcy's body. She shook in humiliating arousal. Familiar with her sweet scent, there was no doubt in Tim's mind. *She's orgasming from my hand!*

The moment his stepdaughter finished cumming, he lifted her off his lap. Returning her into bed, he ran from the room. Both stepfather and daughter were left in shame. While one curled up in a ball on her bed, the other dropped upon his bedroom floor.

While Darcy was left to ponder her enjoyment of the act, the senior doctor masturbated into a pair of her stolen panties. Both spent sleepless nights wondering how they'd face each other again. However, a bigger question occupied their minds.

What would tomorrow bring?

*****

Darcy entered the Abel Medical Group office. Spooked from the prior night, she had no plans on telling Sean about it. Not only would it enrage the younger doctor, but it would incriminate her own enjoyment of the act. The orgasm confused her. *Does that mean I want him too? But I never thought about my stepfather like that...well, not until last night, at least.* She put on her gown, entering the gyno chair. Putting her feet in the stirrups, she waved at her stepbrother. "Hi, Sean."

"Hey, beautiful," he said, smiling back at her. Much looser than the other appointments, he seemed comforted in his father's absence. Knowing that Dr. Tim Abel was out to lunch, he was safe from workplace discipline.

Dr. Sean Abel snapped on latex gloves. Taking a seat between his stepsister's stirrup spread thighs, his mouth watered as much as her pink kitty. He said, "Today we'll do a final test, pushing your limits beyond even a penis. If you feel no pain, you're officially cured."

Darcy nodded, both nervously and sexually awaiting the action. She had no idea how far he'd push her, though was excited to find out. Right as Sean spread her, a surprise entered the room.

"Dad?" Sean asked in disbelief.

"Step-dad!" Darcy parroted.

The senior doctor, Tim Abel, shut the door behind him. Darcy quickly pulled her gown closed, covering her juicy fruit. Tim addressed his son. "Since you defied my orders, I'll just have to implement the next measure of discipline."

"You're firing me?" Sean asked.

"I'll be observing you," Tim Abel announced. "To ensure nothing unethical happens in here. Your *relationship* creates a conflict of interest."

Sean's face tightened in stubborn anger. "Fine," he said. "Then you're just in time to see your stepdaughter cured of Vaginismus."

Tim Abel stiffened. Having read the charts, he knew Darcy's issue. However, he expected his son to back down, perform a non-invasive exam instead. To Tim's surprise, Sean would soon stretch and stuff his patient.

Adding a line of lube to Darcy's sticky honey hole, Sean ordered, "We're going to start with a two finger test. I want you to guide them inside you...like last time."

The trembling girl gazed at her peeping stepfather. Sitting in the chair, Tim was tense and uncomfortable. *I think his head's gonna explode,* she silently observed. Awkward or not, her doctor stepbrother currently called the shots. Reaching out, she held her stepbrother's hand. Slowly leading him forward, she aimed Sean's extended fingers toward her pink bull's-eye.

Making contact, the double digits entered the vulnerable girl. With every forward inch, the latex fingers delved deeper into the heavenly haven. Although Darcy's breath thickened, face tensed, it wasn't pain on display. Fully embracing the pleasurable feeling, Darcy was clearly ready to be pushed further.

"Any pain?"

"No, doctor," Darcy said.

"Good. Now, I'll lead the rest," he announced.

The rest? Dr. Tim Abel wondered. *How many fingers will he use?*

Sean slid a third latex finger into the sultry slit. Darcy's breath heaves became more visible, legs tightened. "Pain?"

"No," she repeated.

With just two fingers left, Sean added his pinky. The curvy redhead's reactions became more animated; ass squirmed upon the gyno chair's edge. She was stretched wider than she'd ever been.

Harder than stone, Dr. Tim Abel watched in lustful jealousy. Seeing the ambition in his son's eyes, he was almost impressed by the young doctor's courage. As much as he wanted to stop the exam, something inside him yearned to see his stepdaughter medically fisted.

"I need you to take a very deep breath," Sean ordered Darcy. This will likely hurt a little...embrace the pain."

Darcy's body shook, feeling her stepbrother's gloved thumb complete the package. Gasping loudly, the redheaded patient grasped the chair rails. Slowly, carefully and absolutely, Dr. Sean Abel's full hand stretched Darcy's steaming sex.

Once inside, he formed a fist. Pushing deeper into the gaping glory hole, his glove slid to her growing depths. Sean's wrist reached wet flesh, smearing exposed skin. The unbelievable pressure sent Darcy into instant, unexpected orgasm.

Writhing in her chair, the spread patient shook like a sexual epileptic. The heaviness inside her aroused every nerve within. Her

G-spot throbbed, choked of life, squeezed to a near bursting point. Biting her bottom lip, Darcy covered her mouth. All control left her. Her body hijacked her mind, pushing and heaving downward.

Sean felt powerful, as if delivering vengeance for the past. He intended to challenge the senior doctor's authority, sick of being treated like a child. However, the more he thought about it, he realized his career would pay the price. He didn't dare stare over at his father, fearful that his boss may fist his face instead. Sean sensed the drooling, zombified look Tim wore.

Suddenly, Sean's latex fist was forced from his stepsister's creamy chasm. A stream of sticky liquid squirted from Darcy's pink palace. Sean's face was in the blast zone, covered in a geyser of G-spot fluid.

He tasted her, drinking the sweet spray. As the human shower stopped, he licked his lips. Darcy's pussy snapped in quivers and contractions. She slowly came back to earth, realizing, *Oh shit! Did I just cum in front of my stepfather? He'll really kill Sean now! Maybe me too!* Tilting her head toward the man, she saw his beet red face. Though, a strained hard cock was evident as well.

Realizing he'd soon be in trouble, Sean completed the exam. "Was there any pain?"

"It was a good pain, doctor," Darcy said.

"You're cured, Ms. Smith."

"That's enough!" Tim Abel finally managed to speak. Standing, he shouted, "Go home, Doctor."

"I did my job...nothing more," Sean defended.

"I said go home now!"

"So that's it? I'm no longer employed in the practice?"

"I need to think about *that*. You're suspended without pay until I say so."

Rage crossed Sean's face. "Fine," he responded, exiting the room.

"Umm...I'll get dressed now," an uncomfortable Darcy said, standing to grab her clothes. She paused, waiting for her stepfather to leave. He didn't. Instead, the man stayed, quietly watching her.

Too fearful to ask his exit, she quickly dropped her gown. Standing fully nude before her aroused and angered stepfather, the curvy redhead shielded her fabulous femininity. She only had so many hands. Putting on each layer of clothing, her hourglass shape was revealed to Tim more.

Conflicted between step-family and sex, patients and lovers, doctors and ethics, Tim Abel remained silent.

"I'll go now," Darcy said, creeping toward the door.

"Wait," he said.

"I'm in trouble?"

"No."

"Why not? I mean...not that I wanna be. Please don't blame Sean...this is my fault too."

"I need you to return tomorrow."

"Here?"

"Yes."

"I thought you told Sean not to come in?"

"I did."

Then who'll examine me?"

After a long, thought-out pause, Dr. Tim Abel said, "I will."

CHAPTER FOUR

Dr. Tim Abel's heart pounded. The man faced sickness and disease every day, performing countless high-pressure procedures. However, the thought of examining his stepdaughter made him jitter like a flu patient.

His stomach wanted to upchuck while his cock begged to cum. For every imagined regret, an erotic scenario rivaled it. *Can I really cross an ethical line with a patient? Hell, can I do that with my own stepdaughter? Shit, I'm not doing it. I'll inform her tomorrow,* he thought.

Damn me! I must do this, his mind quickly changed. *If not for sex...then for sanity. All these damn years of inner-emptiness has taken a toll. The reason my heart hasn't healed...has to lie with Darcy! If she's the only cure, I owe it to myself. When my wife died...I thought my love died with her. It appears one last chance may exist...with her daughter. My son will understand someday.*

Returning to his thoughts, Tim's mind was made up. He knew his plan of attack would have to be powerful. *Sean's already made her vaginally orgasm. So, I have to raise the bar...break new sexual ground. I may only have one shot at this. By the time she leaves my gyno chair, she must question everything she feels for my son. Her pleasure must outweigh societal judgment. A stepbrother is still less taboo than a stepfather. I laid with her mother sexually! Man, my odds are steep. She's worth the risk...so is my future happiness.*

Now I have to hope she shows up.

*****

I'm not going tomorrow, Darcy thought, tossing and turning in her bed. She couldn't sleep, plagued by a conflicted mind. Her night was as restless as the man in the next room. *What choice do I have? If I say no, he can kick me out of the house, not pay for college. If I say yes, I'll have to be naked and touched by my stepfather. Nipples...go down now!* She ordered her perky red darts. Unfortunately, they had a mind of their own, reacting to the latter sexual scenario. As much as the redhead denied it, the thought of the handsome older man got her hot. The taboo was even greater than Sean's examinations.

What will he do to me? What if it's not sexual at all...but really just a check-up? Then nothing bad happens, Sean gets his job back, and we live happily ever after. But what if it IS sexual? Do I tell my stepbrother? He won't want me anymore. OMG...what if I DO like it? Forget rejection...I'll be forced to choose between my stepfather and stepbrother! That's crazy! I'm not going...end of story.

At least...I don't think so.

*****

"Put on this gown...take a seat in the gyno chair. Dr. Abel will be right in to see you," the nurse said, exiting the room.

I'm such a coward! Darcy thought, breaking her own promise not to show for the appointment. She slowly peeled off her clothes, putting on the paper medical gown like a prison uniform. Every step of the way she was ready to run out screaming. Though, a force kept her there. It was truth.

Deny it or not, she always felt strongly for the man. Much like her stepbrother, she once looked upon Tim Abel in youthful admiration. Though thrust into a world of adulthood, her definition of love merged with lust. By day's end, Darcy would never gaze upon her stepfather with the same eyes.

The door opened, no knock preceded it. Stiff and unsure, the 54 year-old doctor entered the room. They shared a millisecond stare, both turning away in awkwardness. "How are you today...Ms. Smith?" Tim asked coldly.

OK, so maybe he'll stay doctorly after all. I can live with this. "I'm good, doctor. Like...*totally* healthy."

He flipped through her chart, sticking to the medical script. "So...my partner treated you for Vaginismus. Would you say the pain has fully subsided?"

"Yeah, doctor. Totally cured."

"Good. Unfortunately, this type of issue rarely stops in one bodily area."

"Huh?"

"The same mental fears which caused your Vaginismus...may present themselves during other sexual acts."

"Oh it's ok...I just won't do those dirty things."

"Maybe not currently...but you'll want to...in time. Therefore...I'll *test* those areas."

"Test? Please tell me it's a written test, doctor."

"No, Ms. Smith...it's a physical one."

"Damn."

"Don't worry...just relax. As quickly as you were cured of the Vaginismus...I have no doubt of your full triumph."

"What other areas will you test?"

"Your gag reflex...for one. Anal tension and development as well."

"Holy hell...did you say...*anal*?"

"It'll all be worth it in the *end*," he said cryptically. "Once you learn to get past the pain...you'll make a man very happy someday."

The doctor's words made Darcy's body tingle with lust. She was always fairly submissive to her stepfather, but the idea of sexual submission was new, exciting and scary.

He snapped on a pair of latex gloves, announcing, "Place your feet in the stirrups, Ms. Smith."

Darcy's apprehensive thighs slowly spread for her step-doctor. Tim Abel's mouth watered at the sight of a soaked slit, tempted by the scent of her pleasure. He thirsted for her taste like his son did.

Sneaking between his stepdaughter's thighs, he grabbed a small tongue depressor. "I'll start with a gag reflex test."

"I'd guess gag reflex like in...throat? Since I don't think my butt hole gags." Darcy said.

"Throat would be correct. I'll use this tongue depressor to stimulate your glands."

"OK, I see why they call it *depressing*. Dr. step-dad...I thought you were an OB-GYN? Do you even deal with the mouth?"

The quick thinking doctor said, "I'm an OB-GYN & T."

"What's the T stand for?"

"Throat," he said coyly. "Now...open wide and say...ahhhh."

Seeing the flat wooden stick approach her, she had no choice but to obey. Her mouth opened, tongue extended, "Ahhhh."

Wasting no time, Dr. Tim Abel snuck the depressor to the back of Darcy's tongue. A thick gag sounded from the redheaded patient's throat. Her mouth closed, chomping on the wooden stick.

He pulled it out from her closed jaw. "Exactly what I suspected," he said, reaching for a metal contraption.

"What did you expect?"

"You're a gagger."

"Is that curable?"

"Lucky for you...it is," he said, strapping a dental gag to her head.

"What's this for?"

Before verbally answering, Dr. Abel hooked Darcy's lips with the steel contraption. Her mouth was instantly stretched open like a blowup doll. She tried to remove it, reaching for the gag. He grabbed her hands, returning them to the chair rails. Using medical tape, he bound her wrists to it.

Unable to properly speak, Darcy grunted. The harder she tried, the more saliva pooled in her mouth. Her stepfather continued. "Doctor's office or not...I still reserve the right to discipline my stepdaughter," he announced. Grabbing the tongue depressor, he slid the stick into her throat.

A chorus of feminine gags exited, greater than before. Dr. Abel instructed, "Relax your tongue completely...so it goes flat." The fearful redhead continued gagging, ignoring her stepfather's advice. Tim kept the depressor in-place, saying, "You can panic and do it your own way...continue gagging...or submit to me. Your choice."

Since eternal gagging wasn't an option, Darcy was forced to comply. Fighting the pressured feeling, she obeyed. Her gags still continued, though calmed greatly. Dr. Abel nodded, "Good girl...much better." Removing the wooden stick, he reached for a dilator. The redhead's eyes widened, no stranger to the plastic invader.

She squirmed, unable to break free. All she could do was hold still, as her stepfather took aim for her mouth. Before the dilator, he stuck two latex fingers deep into her throat. A massive gag erupted, forcing a stream of sweet saliva down her chin. "Remember what I said...relax your tongue completely...let it go limp. Include your throat and neck tension too."

Obeying her step-doctor, the gags calmed, though still came. Tim's free hand grasped Darcy's throat, squeezing hard with his latex glove. The choking action brought more gags, confusing the patient to its purpose. However, when Dr. Abel released neck tension, the redhead felt the difference. Her throat naturally relaxed.

The gags stopped even more, sputtering occasionally, but rare. Removing his fingers, he grabbed the dilator again. It's girth and length resembled a smaller penis. Darcy trembled, feeling her body shake with sexual anticipation. Her stepfather's dominance turned her on.

Using his right hand, Tim Abel placed the plastic phallus to his stepdaughter's tongue. While it slowly entered her mouth, the doctor's left hand returned to her throat. Simultaneously, the dilator deep-throated her and the step-doctor choked her. A muffled gag exited Darcy's mouth, body froze in submission.

Knowing she couldn't fight it, she applied her stepfather's advice. First, she fully relaxed her tongue. Next, she focused on the hand choking her throat. The moment Tim's tension was released, the curvy patient let all stiffness go. Her mouth and throat fully submitted to her stepfather.

As the gagging stopped, the dilator took on newfound ease. Tim pumped the plastic invader in and out. When it touched Darcy's tender throat, the step-doctor simply retightened his chokehold, forcing her to recognize the tension.

Loosening his grasp again, he watched the redhead relax, allowing him deeper oral access. He continued it for another ten minutes, waiting until she was gag-free. Getting harder with each moment, he imagined his cock face-fucking Darcy's virgin mouth. There was no turning back at that point. As far as he'd pushed her, an oral invasion was coming. The question was when to attempt it.

A gentle stream of saliva trickled from Darcy's stretched lips. Removing the dilator and neck grasp, Dr. Abel collected a pool of the natural lubricant upon his rubber glove.

Finally! Can you get this thing off me now? I feel like a caught fish! Darcy silently thought. She tried to say as much, only managing a bunch of gurgling noises.

However, the doctor moved downward instead. Crouching between her spread thighs, he left the dental gag in-place. He also kept her wrists bound to the armrests. Avoiding her sopping wet pussy, he pressed a latex finger to her asshole.

Darcy's ass cheeks tensed, trying to ban the anal enemy from crashing her guarded gates. Fighting beyond a worthy muscular defense, Tim Abel pressed inward. His stiffened digit slowly entered the stepdaughter's asshole.

A deep moan snuck from Darcy's stretched mouth. The deeper the doctor's finger went, the tighter her sphincter got. Before he could fully enter, her anal grip stopped him cold. He couldn't force it any further.

Dr. Abel ordered his patient, "I need you to tighten your cheeks even more...as hard as you can. Squeeze my finger with your anus."

Already very tense, Darcy applied all pressure to her backside. Tim Abel grimaced, feeling his finger flattened by his stepdaughter's ass. He refused to withdraw, knowing it would help her in the long run. After waiting a full minute, he announced, "Now let your hold go!"

The curvy redhead went limp, allowing the doctor to enter knuckle deep. Fully inside her forbidden flume, the redhead quickly tightened again. "Quick, small breaths," he instructed her.

Still dental gagged, Darcy obeyed. With each breath, her anal grip loosened more. Eventually, her ass became accustomed to its new guest, allowing her to accept it. She was finally able to focus on inner-sensation. Feeling her hold lighten, Tim Abel removed his finger.

Reaching for a small dilator plug, he moved up toward her opened mouth. Sliding it inside the warm, wet orifice the doctor lubed it to a saturation point. Sitting back down, Tim placed the plastic to Darcy's warmed hole.

Feeling her cheeks tense again, Tim said, "Like before...tighten hard."

The redheaded patient submissively obeyed, drifting into a near sub-space coma. Her buns turned to steel, body directed all its energy into one part. In the process her vaginal palace dripped with newfound wetness.

"Now relax! Breaths!"

No longer able to keep the tension, Darcy let her guard down. The butt plug immediately conquered his stepdaughter's ass. Her body shook, feeling the short nub fill her backside. Up to its beveled edge, the plug was secured, held in place by the redhead's increased anal tension.

She wiggled in her tape restraint, feeling a discomforting stretch of her virgin asshole. The sensitive anal nerves burned, awaiting an

tightened, choking the plastic invader harder. She felt like she'd soon pass out when the step-doctor released his hold.

All air returned, allowing her to fully relax. Wasting no time, Dr. Abel formed a steady rhythm, fucking her mouth. All 8-inches claimed her tongue, balls smacking Darcy's pillowy lips. With the gagging under control, the stepfather reached down behind himself. His latex covered hands slid to his stepdaughter's clit. Pinching the love button between his fingers, he rubbed in circles. Then, he slid a finger in her pussy, alternating between dual sensations.

Darcy inhaled deeply, ingesting more of the doctorly offering. At that moment, her ass, vaginal palace, and mouth were stimulated at once. The anal pain heated to an intense pleasure, her mind unable to distinguish between them both.

Feeling his cock flooded, Tim pumped his stepdaughter's mouth harder. Crashing into her face, he felt his shaft swell with sperm. A liquid eruption neared, boiling within. Grabbing her red hair, he forced her head into him. Suddenly, he grunted, releasing a creamy treat into his patient's mouth. The curvy redhead felt pale streams enter her throat.

Filled faster than she could control, all she could do was swallow stepfather sperm. No other option was offered. The taste slowly seeped into her buds. What was first savory soon turned sweet, causing the stepdaughter to crave more.

Manly grunts filled the air, as Dr. Abel yanked on his fistful of red hair. Pressing her dental gagged mouth deep into his balls, his opposite hand still finger fucked her pussy. Two fingers crashed her pink slit, putting more pressure on the anal plug. Pounded in double penetration, Darcy broke in orgasm.

Her nubile curves trembled in fits of cold heat. While she tingled with radiant sparks, her mouth kept swallowing more manly deposits. Tim thought, *This is insane! I'm cumming in my stepdaughter's mouth!*

Darcy's thoughts were similar. *I'm swallowing stepfather sperm! This is sooooo wrong...but soooooooooo HOT!*

Both slowly simmered, as Dr. Abel crashed upon Darcy's chest. Both remained quiet, not knowing what to make of the moment. The step-doctor released his patient from her gag and bonds. The redhead was surprisingly in no hurry to leave. She oddly wanted more cum.

"Leave the plug in...until tonight," Dr. Abel instructed.

"What happens tonight?" Darcy asked.

"We'll test your anal response as well...with the real thing," he said.

"Here?" she wondered.

"No...at home."

Oh shit! We're taking this into the bedroom now? Does this mean...he wants more than just sex? It's like crossing a line! But what about Sean? I mean, he did say we could see other people...we're not officially together...but what if feelings form for step-dad too? Do I have to choose between both? Do I tell Sean about this? He'll go nuts! Damn...as if this wasn't complicated enough! Will this plug really stay in my butthole until tonight?

"Get dressed," Dr. Abel said. "I will see you tonight, Ms. Smith."

*****

The curvy redhead hobbled toward the house. To her horrific shock, stepbrother Sean awaited at the door. *Oh no! Try not to wobble...like you have a plug up your ass!*

She cringed, exiting the car. By the first step, she'd given up on her mission to fool him. Feeling the plug stretch her hole, her expression wouldn't be easy to hide.

"Where've you been?" Sean asked.

"I was kinda held up by an...*asshole*. The morning certainly *sucked*," she cringed, realizing her poor choice of revealing words.

"Where were you? What asshole are you referring to?"

"Oh...don't worry about it," she said, opening the door. Wobbling to her bedroom, Sean studied the odd sway of Darcy's ass.

"Did dad mention me today?"

"*Dad*? Why are you asking me? Why would I see *him* this morning?" she asked nervously.

"Before he left for work. You *do* live together," Sean said.

"Oh...right. He didn't mention you," she said, entering her room.

Sean followed, expecting her to sit on the bed. Instead, she plopped down like a felled tree. He asked, "What's wrong? Did you pull something?"

Just my stepfather's penis...ugh...he's gonna kill me! "Nope...didn't pull on anything."

"I mean...your back...or side...or *backside*," he suspiciously fished. "Let me take a look," he said, moving in toward her.

"Uh...no, I'd rather you didn't."

"Come on...no playing bashful with me now. I've obviously seen your goods," he said, flipping her over. In one swoop, Darcy's secret was out. Her pants and underwear came down, revealing an inserted plastic butt-plug. "*Dad*...did this? He wouldn't dare!"

"He dared...I didn't wanna be examined by him, but...I kinda had to."

"It's why he suspended me...so he could get *you* in the gyno chair instead!"

"Maybe."

"Well...lets see him stop *this*," Sean said, attempting to remove the butt-plug.

"Don't!" she begged.

"Why not? You like it?"

"No! It's just...well, it's for my anal development. A good cause."

"Wait...did he have sex with you?"

"No. Well, it kinda depends what the definition of *sex* is."

"Don't go Clinton on me! Some type of sex was had! Admit it!"

She blushed, quickly pulling up her pants. Standing up, she said, "I didn't mean to like it."

"So you *did* like it!" he shouted in sickness.

"I'm sorry, Sean...the butt play plus the oral worked on me."

"He gave you oral?"

"No...the other way around."

"Oh shit! Did he cum in your mouth?"

"Maybe."

"Did you swallow?"

"A little."

"There's no *little* when it comes to swallowing...you did or did not!"

"I did," she said shamefully.

"You swallowed stepfather sperm...do you realize how twisted that is?"

"Well you squirted stepbrother sperm in my pussy! Is that not as nuts?"

"Don't throw this back on me! *You* cheated!"

"No I didn't! Sean, you told me to see others...that *we* weren't a couple!"

"Those *others* didn't include my fucking father!"

"You act like I planned it!"

"What matters is you enjoyed it! Was he better than me?"

"No! Besides...you two didn't even do the same things."

"Oh so it's a competition now...I guess you'll need to try us both out first? Not happening!"

"I never said that!"

"Make your decision...which one do you want? You can't have both!"

"Ugh! Are we really in a stepbrother, stepfather, stepdaughter love triangle? I thought this crap only happened in eBooks!"

"Look, I was wrong by telling you to see others. I was a fool...letting my reputation take precedence over my heart. Darcy, I love you...more than a stepsister. I love you like a wife."

The redhead gasped. "Really?"

"Yes. I need to know if you feel the same."

"I do," she said positively.

"OK, then tell dad your decision tonight. Let him down easily."

"But..."

"But what?" he asked in a worried tone.

"I *might* love him too."

"No shit!"

"I don't know what I'm feeling right now, Sean. My head's a mess...I'm confused. I never expected any of this."

"He's an old man! I'm a strapping young doctor in the prime of his life. This is a damn ego blowing insult."

"Exactly...you can have any girl you want...so why me? How do I know you won't just freak out again...dump me?"

"Because...I wouldn't do that to you. I need to know now...do you love me or him? Not in a family way...in a sexual way. Decide."

Placing her head in hands, tears fell from her eyes. "I need a day...to decide."

He sighed, shaking his head in disgust. "Don't bother. You're indecision speaks loud enough," he said, heading toward the exit.

"So you're saying we're done?"

Pausing before exiting her room, Sean said, "I'm saying...I hope he treats you well...like the beautiful girl you are." He left the room.

"No, Sean!" she called to him. "Don't go...I'm sorry. I don't want to lose you...I love you too!"

Long gone before Darcy's confessed love, Sean exited the front door. The redhead crashed upon her bed, thoughts tearing through her mind. *I can't believe this is happening! How could I choose between two men I love so much? I mean, I love them both in different ways...I just don't know which way to go. Now, I may not*

CHAPTER FIVE

Tim Abel entered his home, exhaling deeply. *Did today really happen or is this just a dream?* Heading toward his bedroom, he saw Darcy's light on. In just a few hours, he'd be inside her.

Entering the shower, he let hot water cascade his face. *I don't understand it,* he thought to himself. *I loved cumming in her mouth...it felt damn good...sexually. Though, I'm still hollow inside. Emptiness, loneliness...I expected it all to just lift...by being with her. She was supposed to heal my heart, return the loss of her mother. Maybe once I enter her...my humanity will return. I can only hope.*

Freshly bathed, he put on silk boxer shorts, leaving his shirt off. He paused at his stepdaughter's door, opening it. Entering, salt and pepper chest hair covered strong pecks and abs. Although Darcy saw her stepfather at the pool or in a towel, she took new notice. *He's kinda in hot shape.*

Beforehand, she'd nervously sat, gazing at her phone aimlessly. Every moment that ticked, she anxiously awaited his summons of her. Wearing just a short nightshirt, no panties were underneath. She'd wondered, *Will we do it in here? Will it just be anal?*

Her first question was soon answered. He walked to the bed, lifting her into a cradle carry. She hugged his neck, hanging on tight. His cologne was sharp, hold secure. Feeling helpless in his arms, she fully submitted to him.

Carried into the hallway, her red slit and ass cheeks peeked from the short covering. Her stepfather led her to the master bedroom. Darcy gasped, seeing the King-sized mattress he'd made love to her mother on. It was suddenly apparent; she'd soon cum in *that* same bed.

Stepfather Tim, placed Darcy on silk sheets. Her body went limp, softly sinking into the plush surface. Not knowing where he'd start, she was pleasantly greeted with a kiss upon her lips. The feeling was more than erotic, it was sensual. More than lust, she felt love. *If this is what my mother felt everyday, she was one lucky woman.*

Before he made another move, he said, "I know you have feelings for your stepbrother too, I'm sorry for making this harder on you. I just had to..."

"I'm glad you did, step-dad."

Suddenly realizing her shared feelings, Tim decided to take it a step further. "I'm in love with you, Darcy...at least, I think I am. I need to know if you feel the same...before we do this."

"I do...well, I think I do. I've never been in love before...especially not with step-family. I don't know what I'm feeling. The whole thing is new to me."

He smiled, "You can count me in on that. I just want to tell you, if you choose Sean, I'll understand."

"Thank you," she said in relief.

"However, I have to say this...no matter how much it pains me to compete with my son."

"OK."

"For all his youth and stamina, *I'm* the one who's already proven my love. I'm the one who's always provided for you...protected you. You saw the undying love I had...*still* have...for your mother."

"I see it in your eyes," she said, gazing into the man's experienced stare. Though as much as she admired it, she wondered if it was an asset or hindrance. *Does he really love me...or my mother through me?*

He leaned in for another sensual kiss. His lips drifted down her neck, kissing further downward. He pulled her nightshirt at the neck, stretching it down her shoulders. Darcy's braless C-cups sprang out, licked by her stepfather's tongue.

He gnawed upon her tender nipple, sending a spiraling jolt of lust down her spine. Her sweet slit dripped, ass throbbed with pained pleasure. The 54-year-old doctor kissed 18-year-old skin, passing his stepdaughter's soft belly. Licking straight down her soaked snatch, his tongue drank its fill.

Darcy's gentle moans exited her lungs feeling her stepfather arrive at her stuffed ass. Rimming around the plug's end, Tim made the curvy redhead squirm. Removing the plug, a large gaping hole awaited conquering.

The senior doctor removed his boxers. His 8-inch arrow aimed right for its anal target. Even stretched, he lubed her with his saliva, licking around and within her ticklish ass. Once it was fully soaked, the doctor placed his cock head to hole. Pressing forward, he entered Darcy's forbidden garden.

Although it was looser than pre-plug tension, the virgin ass was still quite tight. Having not had anal since his deceased wife, Tim gasped at the intense grip around his rod. As the head passed the anal ring, Darcy stiffened more. "Like in the exam room...tighten hard...then let go. Short, quick breathes."

The submissive stepdaughter obeyed, squeezing her round cheeks. Feeling his cock squashed, Tim grabbed onto her hips, scraping his nails into her skin. After a minute, Darcy relaxed, offering a moment of limpness.

Feeling her defenses fall, Dr. Abel plunged deep into her abyss. He got halfway in before she tightened again. Heat blazed her backside, sensitive sexual nerves were awakened in new ways. The step-doctor pushed forward aggressively, taking the fight to his stepdaughter's asshole. *Her ass will be mine! After that...I'll claim her womb!*

His spit-soaked cock sank inside the canal, soon landing balls deep. Darcy cried out, feeling an anal stretch much greater than the plug. In fact, it was a sensation so powerful it crossed physical, mental and emotional lines. Her body shook, beads of sweat sailed down her skin.

Ready to begin pumping her, stepfather Tim wrapped her in secure arms. The first thrust began, outward slowly, inward fast and furiously. Another moan sounded from Darcy. Her cry was less pain, more pleasure, absorbing the electric buzz from head to toe.

With each new anal invasion, she embraced intensity more. Dr. Abel lifted his stepdaughter's legs into the air, resting her feet upon his shoulders. He crashed into her, lower abs smacking the wet slit and engorged clit. Darcy felt herself soaking the sheets. Her love juice baptized the bed like her mother before.

I must seed her! Impregnating her will ensure she's mine. But...this ass feels too good to withdraw. I must not cum...somehow! He warned himself. However, that battle was closer to being lost with every thrust. Feeling a hot stream of cum climb his shaft, he kept risking another dip.

A manly grunt filled the air, driven beyond human control. Milked of all his worth, Darcy's stepfather erupted prematurely. The older man unloaded heavily, filling the virgin canal with hot spunk.

Feeling her backend sprayed with sperm, the curvy redhead exploded in her own pleasure. Different than prior vaginal bliss, the orgasm was fully anal. A good burn ached her asshole, cooled with constant streams of stepfather seed.

The two banged away until their spasms stopped. Tim Abel crashed into his stepdaughter's chest, laying his head upon her. They held each other, laying silent in reflection. Tim's cock remained in ass until flaccid. A sea of sperm seeped out, soaking the bed more.

Darcy felt amazing, knowing she had a lot to think about. Even though Sean broke up with her, she had to weigh their strengths and weaknesses. She had to gauge her future as well as her present. The only thing she was currently sure about was the decision's difficulty.

Tim Abel felt equally as pleased. Her pressed his head into her young breasts, absorbing the forgotten feeling of passionate sex. However, as the eroticism began to fade, his heart remained heavy. Much like his stepdaughter, he wasn't sure what he felt. He was even less sure, what to do.

✳✳✳✳✳

A new light of day streamed through window-blinds. Darcy awoke from a deep sleep, wondering if the anal antics were just a dream. Her sore asshole and stepfather's bed proved its reality.

Though an even bigger surprise was the missing. "Step-dad? Are you home?" she called out. No answer arrived. Being the weekend, she knew he wasn't at work. *He must be out already*, she told herself. Left alone with her thoughts, she welcomed the quiet time.

Throughout her shower, she debated both mens' strengths and weaknesses. *Sean...strong points. He's hot, closer to my age, great sex, similar music likes, and not gonna need a hip replacement by the time I'm 30. If we have kids, he'll live longer to watch them grow up, and his sperm probably swims better. The man gives me butterflies just by being near. Weak points...he's my stepbrother. He's hot! I know I called that a strong point, but he examines sexy patients...I'll look like dog meat to him. He may not want to settle in marriage, I do. Oh yeah, and one more thing...he dumped me yesterday. Bottom line...he's amazing boyfriend material, but is he husband material?*

Darcy grasped her red hair with both hands, tugging on it in a stressed out manner. Her thought process continued. *My step-dad...strong points. He's handsome, smart, protective, successful, rich, trust worthy and a good listener. Weak points, He's my step-dad. Less in common with me. He's mature to my immature. Once had all kinds of sex with my mom. Bottomline...he'll marry me, not cheat on me. Is that really true love? Is it fair to marry him because he's safe?*

"Ugh!" Darcy shouted loudly. Looking to the sky, she asked, "Mom...it's days like this I wish you were here to help me! Of course, you'd be married to one of the men...and the debate would be over...but that's beside the point! Wait...that's it!" she realized. "Although you can't come to me...I can go to you!"

*****

Darcy arrived at the cemetery, a place she once visited daily. Although visitation lessened in time, the spirit of the place never left her memory. She was able to think, reflect, and even talk to her mother. Walking down the aisle of stones, such a moment was exactly what she needed.

Looking downward while walking, her head and heart were at war. *I know I should pick my step-dad...it's safe. I mean, if my stepbrother breaks my heart...things will be forever awkward. So why do I want him so bad then? He excites me...keeps me on my toes. Step-dad calms me, but I'm young...I wanna dive into life's deep-end, not shallow pool. It's wrong to love someone...just to not get hurt. But...how do I tell him that? He'll be crushed...disown me. Maybe he'll even fire Sean!*

She hoped for a motherly sign. Although she didn't expect one, she always imagined little things like fallen branches or wind gusts as unworldly communication. Of course, she never expected an actual voice.

"Darcy."

The redhead looked up from her slump, seeing her mother's grave. Her stepfather stood before it. "Step-dad? How'd you know I'd come here?"

"I didn't. I came here to think."

"Me too. I guess we used to come a lot. I've kinda slacked over the years."

"It's OK. To be honest, I've stayed away myself. Too painful. I honestly believed it would numb the hurt...heal me. It didn't do a damn thing."

She hugged her stepfather, "Me too, dad."

"You called me, dad. After the things we did last night...maybe it would be good to add the *step*-part back. Just for our own sanity."

"Good point," she said, staring down at the granite grave. "Do you mind...if I ask what you were thinking?"

He paused. "Ladies first."

"You can probably guess."

"Love."

"Yeah. I know this sounds dumb...but I kinda feel guilty. Like I need mom's permission or something."

"No, that sounds quite accurate. I'm here to do the same."

"Really? I thought I was the only wacko to talk to her here."

"I talk to her everywhere...this place just seems like she can hear me. More importantly, it's like she'll answer me back. Maybe it's the quiet...a rarity in today's world of digital distractions."

"True. Can I ask...if she answered you?"

After a long pause and deep sigh, he said, "She didn't need to tell me...what I already knew."

"Which is?"

"To step aside...for your good. You belong with a Dr. Abel...just not me."

"You don't love me?" she asked in rejected hurt.

"I do love you," he said. "Like I've always loved you...like a daughter. Minus the anal, of course."

She kissed him on the cheek. "I hope nothing's changed between us...I mean, the naughty things were done with my step-dad...but the man who raised me...is my dad, nothing less."

He put his arm around her shoulder. "Thank you, my red rose."

"Can I ask one more thing?"

"Anything."

"Did you not like...the things we did together? Was I...bad in bed?"

"Not at all! You were...amazing! In every way! It wasn't the sex that caused me to walk away...it wasn't you."

"What was it?"

"It was me. I expected your love to cure me...take the pain away. It wasn't fair to you...or my son. The truth is...I see the way you look at him. It's love, passion...the way I looked at your mother. You deserve that...so does Sean."

"So what happens to you now? You just give up trying to heal?"

"I do what all widows do. We survive. I've seen enough grief in this world to know how it works. Time lessens pain...though never heals. In the end, no one will ever replace her loss."

"Step-dad...I know I'm only 18...but 1 wonder...maybe it's not another person who can save you. Maybe the answer isn't love at all."

"If not love, then what? If not me...then who?"

"Yourself," she said, making him think.

"You're growing up, kid. I'm damn proud of the woman you're becoming."

"A good woman...raised by a great man."

He smirked. "A lucky man, I am. We should go," he said, blowing a kiss at his deceased wife's grave. Darcy did the same. As they walked back to their cars, Tim Abel asked, "Do you think my son will ever forgive me?"

"He'll forgive you. It's *me*...he won't forgive."

"Why's he mad at you? He doesn't even know what we did."

"I kinda let the cat outta the bag...or should I say...the dildo outta the butt. He saw it...I admitted liking it. He ended things...even though we weren't even together. I guess it was crazy of me to think it could work anyway. I mean...Did I really believe a stepbrother and stepsister could actually end up together?"

Guilt crossed Tim's face. "Why can't they?"

"Cuz...we'll always have to explain ourselves to someone. The world won't accept it."

"Then let me offer your own advice back. Maybe it's time you live for *yourself*."

"So you support us now?"

"I support love. The relationship's perfectly legal...no blood relation. It's not like you'll give birth to a three-headed baby."

"Ha, exactly what I said! But...Sean will never accept what you and I did. I mean...it's not like you can make him love me again."

"Darcy, trust me...true love doesn't die. I'm living proof of that."

"So what can I do?"

"Be you...and I'll be me."

"His boss?"

"His father. And it's about time I acted like it."

*****

Dr. Sean Abel entered the group practice. Having been suspended a day of work, he had time to think and reflect. *I'm better off without her,* he assured himself. *She's equally better off without me. We'll be called freaks...our kids not accepted, relatives and friends gossiping behind our backs. Then if we break up...our small family unit will be destroyed. I should walk away...let my father finally get his closure. So why can't I? Either way...it's her choice, not mine. She wants my father...and I must accept it...accept them. Like it or not.*

Exhaling, Sean approached the first door, taking the chart. A deep voice sounded from behind. "Dr. Abel...I believe you're at the wrong door."

Turning around in shock, Sean saw his father. "Dad? I mean...Dr. Abel...what are you talking about? This is my wing of the practice. It's my exam room. Is this about...our familial issue? Look, if it stops all this fighting...I'm giving up..."

"*Doctor*...as your boss, my order is final. Today...there will be a change of plans."

"Fine, where do you want me?"

"Where you belong."

"Where's that...if not here?"

"Room 2," Tim said.

Rolling his eyes, Dr. Sean Abel headed for the particular room. Grabbing the folder in anger, he didn't even bother with the name. Opening the door, he entered to a shocking surprise. "Darcy?" he asked.

The redheaded stepsister reclined in the gyno chair. Her feet were in the stirrups, paper gown barely clung to porcelain skin. "Hi, doctor," she said with a wink.

Stunned and speechless, he turned to look back at his father. The senior Dr. Abel waited at the door. He nudged his son forward. "Go...examine your patient, doctor. Examine your stepsister. Examine your true *love*," he said in newfound approval, shutting the door behind him.

A large smile crossed Sean's face, aiming his passionate gaze to Darcy's eyes. Getting his mojo back, he reached for a rubber glove.

Snapping it on his hand, he stepped between the curvy redhead's thick thighs. "So...where should I start?"

"Right here, doctor," Darcy said eagerly, pointing at her lips. The step-doctor leaned in, sealing their step-love-affair with a kiss.

The Step Doctors 2

Seeded by a Step

by

J.D. GRAYSON

28,000 words

All books are now available in Paperback. For autographed copies
please send your request to JDGrayson@hotmail.com

Visit J.D. Grayson's website to signup for a new release alerts.

Website: www.JDGraysonBooks.com

Twitter: @JDGraysonBooks

CHAPTER ONE

Ting, ting, ting, Dr. Sean Abel tapped his champagne glass with a spoon. Standing before a crowd of family members, he wore a pricy suit. His stepsister stood closely beside him, trembling in-place. Her fire-red dress clung to curves like a deadly mountain road. All eyes fixated upon them both. The doctor said, "I'd like to make an announcement."

Six months had passed since Darcy and Sean's relationship became official. Their chemistry got stronger with each moment, sexual passion burned hotter than molten lava. Lust grew into true love, leaving no doubt in their minds: it was time to unite in marriage.

Familiar smiles flashed around the lavish ballroom. It was the annual family reunion. Members of the large Abel clan filled every table in the ballroom. A tradition dating back years, it was a time to catch up on life's events and gossip. A memorable and anticipated event, the current year would be no exception.

Dr. Tim Abel sat at their table, awaiting the expected announcement. He was excited for them, though stressed. Darcy gazed over at her stepfather, unsure if nerves or sadness was glazing his eyes. At that moment, her own nerves were frayed. She warned herself, *Don't vomit on any of them! At least save it until after they're told! It will provide a distraction from the horror!*

The dark-haired, dapper Sean continued with his announcement. "I know many of you wondered when I'd finally man-up...exit bachelorhood. Well, I've finally found the cure."

"Awww," the room gushed and buzzed with excitement. "Who is she?" one member shouted. "Is she here?" yelled another.

Sean lifted his glass into the air. "Please join me in a champagne toast. Let us welcome to the family...actually, she's already *in* the family. My fiancé', Darcy Smith."

The room went dead silent. "Who's that?" A voice echoed throughout the room. "Dear lord...not his...*stepsister!*" said another family member's anguished voice.

Darcy's porcelain skin out shined her dress and hair. A sweating Sean turned to her. She waved at the crowd, numb from fear. *I think they're about to stone me. OK, they don't have stones...but they do have stale dinner rolls. That's just as deadly.*

A laugh echoed across the ballroom, another followed. "It's a joke. He's pulling our legs!" a voice shouted. More laughter joined in on the fun.

Sean grabbed Darcy's hand, holding up her ring finger. Reflected light hit the diamond, blinding their eyes like a sparkling sun. "It's true! I'm going to marry my STEPSISTER! I would've expected a little more class from my family."

"This is sacrilege!" yelled one.

"Gross!" shouted another.

"Three-headed children!" topped it all off. The crowd gasped in horror.

Fury filled Sean's face. "She's NOT blood relation!"

Some formed prayer circles, others shouted curses, a few began to cry. "Burn them at the stake...and I don't mean prime rib!" yelled drunken Uncle Rick.

Darcy whispered, "Sean...let's go. I'm gonna vomit!"

Sean was so fueled with anger he didn't even hear her plea. "Who the hell are you people to judge *us*? We have *actual* criminals, predators, and drug addicts in this family...in this room *tonight*! Shit, I happen to know some of you once voted for Jimmy Carter!"

An even greater gasp of horror filled the room, though no one dared admit such a shameful mistake. "I didn't vote for *him*! *They* did!" many shouted in defensiveness, pointing at other family members.

Sean continued, "You can overlook *those* offenses...but you'll judge me for who I love? It's legal, damn you!"

"Marrying your sister's sick!" drunken Uncle Rick shouted again, getting in Sean's face.

The young doctor's fist tightened, as he bumped chests with the man. Darcy stepped between the two. She tried to push nausea aside, attempting to defuse the situation. "Now, Uncle Rick...you know I'm his stepsister."

"You don't call me step-uncle!" Uncle Rick accused.

"What the hell does *that* prove?" Sean shouted.

"It's proof you're a degenerate! That you're a sicko!" Uncle Rick yelled.

"Yes, I'm really sick...like the vomit kinda sick," Darcy's soft voice evaporated in the shouting.

The two men screamed away, as Dr. Tim Abel rose from his seat. "Stop it now, Rick! You're my brother...they are your nephew and step-niece. You know better than this. You should be ashamed of yourself! In fact, you *all* should be ashamed!"

A hush came over the crowd. The respected doctor was not one to draw attention to himself. When he spoke, people listened. Tim continued, "This is legal...perfectly fine by every rule in the book. Yet, you sit in judgment...because it makes *you* uncomfortable. You all know...I lost the woman I loved...Darcy's mother...to unspeakable tragedy. I'd give my life to save her from that *scumbag*..." Tim paused before finishing. Looking over at Darcy, he remembered, *Watch your words...she doesn't know.* "Save her from the...*driver...*who hit her. You're lucky to find true love once in your life...step or no-step. Sean has *that* love for Darcy...they'll marry, and I'll be proud."

A smile crossed Sean's face, thankful for his father's support and courage. "Thanks, Dad. We're proud to call you *family.*"

The two men nodded at each other. Tim Abel continued on. "And after that...I'll deliver their offspring...my grandchild! And if you people can't deal with that...then we'll take our family unit elsewhere!" He placed his napkin down, pulling out his chair to leave.

Before any move could be made, a drunk Uncle Rick asked, "Will all three heads get a name?" His obnoxious laugh filled the room, followed by others.

Sean's fists tightened, as he prepared to strike his uncle. However, Darcy struck first. *BLURRRRRRRLB!* A stream of projectile vomit sailed from her mouth, decorating Uncle Rick's face. All laughter stopped, as the Abel clan watched in sickened disbelief.

After the jackass uncle was drenched, Sean wiped Darcy's mouth with a cloth napkin. Proudly putting his arm around her, he stood firmly before his familial judges. Tim Abel placed his hands upon their shoulders, pulling them close. "Let's go home."

✳✳✳✳✳

"Do you, Darcy Smith, take Sean Abel to be your lawfully-wedded husband, to have and to hold from this day forward, for better, for worse, for richer, for poorer, in sickness and health, until death do you part?"

"I do," Darcy said sincerely. Her innocent smile beamed, eyes glazed with tears. Although she'd always imagined a fairytale wedding full of guests, none of that mattered anymore. One man held her heart, no fancy frills or decor could change that.

They stood in a beautiful old chapel. Mildewed stones constructed the walls, candles were lit along the sides, wooden beams formed a peaked ceiling, and a faded cross backed a carved alter. The pews were dusty, air musty, and an intimate glow of history warmed their skin.

Their only guest was Darcy's stepfather, standing behind the couple in support. It wasn't a pretentious show as many weddings are. The quickly maturing girl appreciated a very important fact: *This isn't a party...it's a commitment. It's not a room of fakes and drunks whispering gossip and hate...it's the people who matter to me. It's the people I love.*

The priest continued with the vows, turning towards Sean. "And do you, Sean Abel, take Darcy Smith to be your lawfully-wedded wife, to have and to hold from this day forward, for better, for worse, for richer, for poorer, in sickness and health, until death do you part?"

Sean turned to his stepsister, staring into her radiant blue eyes. His momentary silence was not hesitation, but admiration. "I do," he said proudly.

"Then I hereby pronounce you, man and wife, Mr. and Mrs. Abel. You may kiss your bride," the priest said.

Smiles crossed their faces. Moving in toward one another, they shared a passionate kiss. "Congratulations," Tim Abel said from behind.

Sean hugged his father, thankful for the man's support. Next, Tim hugged Darcy. He held her tight, almost desperately. *Is he trembling?* Darcy wondered. *Why? He sounds happy, but something's not right with him lately. Worse than usual.*

As the hug broke, Darcy stared beyond her stepfather's surface-smile. Gazing into his eyes, she saw the same pain which had always been. After their talk at the cemetery, she tried to believe he'd be alright. Though, her thoughts betrayed her willful ignorance. *It's about my mother. This probably reminds him of his own wedding. He still hurts...no matter what I tell myself. I just wish I could help him. I know it's not my fault my love didn't heal his pain. I wish I could heal his heart, help him love again...help him live again. If there was anything I could do...I'd do it.*

*****

The stunning stepsister-wife stood before her new husband. Inside their honeymoon suite, Sean watched in awe. Darcy's red hair lie upon her white satin dress. The two contrasted like fire and ice. Her strapless wedding gown form-fit to every delicious curves. If she had wings, an angel she'd be.

Sean approached the new bride, his strong hands tickled feminine arms. Rising to Darcy's neck, his fingernails teased soft skin. Chills tingled Darcy's body. Slipping his fingers through her hair, the stepbrother-husband massaged her scalp. Moving in toward her mouth, his lips kissed hers. Returning his hungry hands to her wedding gown, he yanked the strapless dress downward. Darcy's slip fell with it.

Braless C-cups were revealed. He smiled at her risqué act. Continuing downward, he rode the undulating coaster from thin-waist to wide-hips. However, instead of continuing to her Promised Land, he stopped.

Why's he stopping? Darcy wondered. *He's seen my body plenty of times...is it no longer hot to him? Is he tired of me? I wonder if stepdad's still game...oh stop! I'm sure he wants me and my crazy insecure self!*

Stepbrother Sean calmed Darcy's fears. Lifting her into strong arms, he laid her on the bed diagonally, so her legs hung off the edge. She sank into the oversized feather bed. Her legs spread, revealing white panties with matching garter stockings.

Tossing his stepsister's shoes away, Sean slid his hands up Darcy's legs. Leaving the stockings in-place, he reached for the underwear. Since they were connected to the garter belt, he tore at the soft crotch cloth instead. Darcy gasped at the hunger in her husband's action. She loved the primal desperation in his eyes, craved more edge. The once innocent virgin was becoming a sex-fiend.

The more silk Sean tore, the more tender red flesh was revealed. Darcy's wet pussy lips showed themselves, along with smooth hairless skin. Her sweet scent hit his nose, enticing stepbrother Sean to ravish his new bride.

He started to move in, as Darcy's voice stopped him. "Sean."

"Something wrong?" he asked in worry.

"No...in fact, everything's right."

"Then why stop me?"

"I wanna have your baby."

"Well...I have to *enter* you for that to happen."

"I know...but...I mean like...*now*."

"Tonight? You realize...storks don't deliver babies, right? It takes time to happen."

She tapped his chest with her foot. "Duh! I just don't wanna wait years. I want a part of you...growing inside me."

"Are you even ovulating?"

"I am."

"How do you know?"

"I Googled it."

He felt her forehead, *Slightly warmer than usual*. The rise in body temperature indicated likely ovulation. "Are you sure you don't want to wait? Live out your youth for a while? What if you discover I'm not a good husband? Do you really want to be tied down like that?"

"You'll be a good husband...like you were a good stepbrother. And Sean...trust me...I wanna be tied down...by you," she said seductively, spreading her legs. "Cum inside me."

The mere words made Sean rock hard. His alpha need to breed was activated. He yanked down his pants, too impatient to unbutton them. A 7-inch cock roared out. It was throbbing, begging to mark its territory upon his stepsister's ovulating womb.

Right before he could enter her, Darcy made another request. "And Sean...uh, would you mind..."

"White coat?"

She blushed, "You know me well. I'm kinda embarrassed to say this...but can we pretend I'm prego...at a gyno appointment. You...and the gyno man...screw me in the gyno chair."

Sean paused in thought. *Gyno as in OBGYN? Is the other man my father? Does she mean him...and me...taking her at once? No way. Just stop thinking and fuck for once!* he chastised himself. Sean dug through his luggage, revealing the white doctor coat. Removing his shirt and tie, a muscular body shined in the room light. Slipping the coat on, its open slit revealed tight abs and a thick manly member.

To Darcy's surprise, Sean revealed a stethoscope and latex gloves as well. He snapped the rubbers on his hands, hanging the scope around his neck. Returning to the bedside, he announced, "The doctor is *in*!"

A large smile crossed Darcy's face. "So hot!"

Darcy pushed out her belly, as if fully pregnant. Stepbrother Sean ran his latex hands along the curved ridge, traveling up to exaggerated breasts. "Tie me," she begged.

Sean gazed around frantically, seeking something to tie his stepsister-wife with. *Phone cords!* He thought. He raced for the room's two phones, yanking the cords from both the receiver and wall-jack. Heading back to his willing captive, he tied one wrist to her raised ankle. Then he tied the other wrist to the other raised ankle. Darcy's feet were forced into the air like stirrups.

He pulled her ass cheeks partially off the bed's side. "Let me lube you," he said, dropping to his knees. Burying his face into her sopping red sea, Dr. Abel licked and sucked at his stepsister's slit. Sean spit inside her, letting it drip down her creamy curtains. She was so wet, beads of feminine rain rolled down Sean's face. Drinking every drop, his throat filled with sweet, sticky pleasure.

He felt the redhead's thighs clamp upon his head. The harder she squeezed, the more juice flowed. Air emptied from Sean's lungs, though he refused to quit. As much as he loved her taste as a girlfriend, somehow she tasted even better as a wife. Darcy finally loosened her thigh grip, legs tired from holding the position.

Forcing himself away from her youthful fountain, stepbrother Sean rose. Darcy focused on the 7-inch cock. She begged, "Please knock me up, doctor! I need your cum in me now!"

Lifting Darcy's tied ankles to his shoulders, the alpha step-doctor was determined to do his manly duty. He moved into her soaked slit, placing his cock at her pink palace. Slowly sinking inside her, he changed into his dominating doctor voice. "Mrs. Abel, I'm going to inseminate you now."

"With your penis, doctor?" she played along. "But what about my husband's sperm?"

"He's shooting blanks...so this job calls for a *real* man's seed," he said confidently, sinking deeper into his stepsister.

Darcy gasped, feeling as if fantasy was reality. All 7-inches entered her, Sean's balls touched her ass cheeks. The redhead was so turned on, her tender tunnel expanded well beyond the doc's cock. The idea of a stepbrother seeding her womb drove her wild with taboo lust.

With Darcy's white-stocking feet upon Sean's shoulders, he kissed and licked them. Moving up her foot's veiled sole, he reached the toes. Engulfing each one in his mouth, he sucked all five tiny digits. Needing to touch flesh, he tore the silky fabric away. Feminine feet were unveiled. Sean's tongue bathed every inch of exposed porcelain skin. The tickling feelings trickled through Darcy's body, making her wetter with each attentive lick. It alone was nearly enough to give her an orgasm.

Stepbrother Sean continued pumping his wife the entire time. Once each inch of foot was worshiped, he took the stethoscope's metal disc in latex hand. He placed it upon her heart. The cold steel contrasted heated skin. Her pores rose in stimulation. A pounding drum beat inside Darcy's body and Sean's ears.

Withdrawing from his newlywed wife's pussy, he spit down upon his cock. Placing it against her tight asshole, it would be his first time claiming her anally. Being well aware that his father conquered her ass first, Sean couldn't go there. However, Darcy still used the dilator to prepare for her future husband's arrival.

Wasting no time, Sean's hard cock pushed into her dark chamber door. Moving slowly, yet aggressively, he popped the anal ring. Plunging deeper, he discovered unknown tightness. His cock ached from her anal grip. He kept pushing, arriving balls deep. Darcy did her breathing exercises, accepting stepbrother cock without complaint.

Soft moans escaped her, the first impalement burning and stretching her hole. After a few more anal strokes, she began to relax. The harder he crashed into her ass, the more her belly naturally protruded. Although she admitted her two doctor fantasy, she didn't dare speak of the man in her mind.

"I'll need another doctor to assist me," he announced, granting Darcy's wish. Sean stuffed two latex fingers in his stepsister's pussy. Then a third and fourth were added. Soon, Darcy was fucked in both holes, cock and fingers. Though in her mind, it was her stepfather's cock joining them.

The curvy redhead felt an orgasmic buzz building within her body. Sean suddenly removed his fingers from the soaked snatch. Although she wanted more, her buzz returned as her step-husband removed the scope. In a bold move, he wrapped the cord around his stepsister's soft neck. Shocked, yet not unpleased, Darcy awaited her husband's action. Putting total trust in him, she went limp in submission.

He tightened the chokehold, constricting her throat, restricting air. Her belly heaved further outward the harder he pulled. All the while, he continued banging away inside his wife's tight ass.

Every muscle in the doctor's arms strained, veins swelled to a popping point. Darcy began choking, struggling for air. However, Sean just erotically strangled her harder. To her shock, the more nervous Darcy was, the hotter and wetter she got. By the time all air was denied her, she'd drenched the bed's edge. Her heart pounded even harder, tied hands reached to remove her husband's hold. The actions were to no avail.

Giving up on fighting it, the stepsister submitted to her husband's dominance. Embracing the edgy act, she zoned-in on the incredible tingling buzz. Dizziness encircled her like a ballet of dark angels. She no longer wanted to stop it, craving the alliance of Sean's plunging cock and harsh erotic asphyxiation.

Just as erotic hypoxia set in, Darcy imagined her stepfather again. She could see him choking her while her stepbrother fucked her. Just then, she exploded into orgasm. Unable to make a sound, her body shook in fits. Fireworks burst inside her mind with streams of reds, yellows, and bright whites.

Sean's alpha need to seed grew more desperate. At that point, his mission traveled well beyond pleasure. He withdrew from ass to pussy, aiming his manly weapon into Darcy's chamber. The stepsister's body tensed so tightly, her spasming pussy forced Sean's cum out.

A loud grunt filled the air, as Sean crashed into Darcy. A blast of white life flooded her birth canal. Thick white streams of heavy seed seeped into the cervix, invading the curvy redhead's womb.

All the while, Sean's choking grip squeezed tighter. The two of them just kept cumming, each entranced by thoughts of fertility. Darcy began to blackout, as Sean's last load soaked her. He released his grip, allowing his stepsister to breathe again. A gush of air filled her lungs, as she desperately replenished the life-giving element.

Sean withdrew, untying his wife's wrists and ankles. He tied her thighs shut, trapping her slit like solid-steel doors. He wasn't letting one ounce of sperm escape her. The couple embraced tightly, each of them imagining their future life together.

Darcy drifted to sleep, picturing birthday parties and family vacations. However, she was woken multiple times by an inserted cock. Like primitive man, Sean fucked her whenever and wherever he wanted. Placed in pile driver and doggie-style positions, the redheaded stepsister was constantly filled with stepbrother cum.

As they both finally settled, Sean couldn't fight a fear from within his mind. *What if I can't impregnate her...my father has cases of infertility every day. What if...the scenario we enacted comes true? What if I was the guy shooting blanks? My pride would be destroyed. I couldn't let some other guy's sperm do the job...they could be a serial killer for all I know. What in the hell would I do?*

*****

Tim Abel stared in the bathroom mirror. A five o'clock shadow peppered his face. Such disorder was uncharacteristic of him, as a clean-shaven face represented professionalism, control. It was crucial that he display such strength to patients. Of course, he hadn't had control of his life since losing his wife.

Rinsing the razor blade with blazing hot water, he touched it to his cheek. Feeling the harsh steel sting, he removed it. He imagined slicing a wrist, letting blood spill everywhere. It was a common fantasy, though the spilled blood was never his. It belonged to someone else.

Placing the razor to his cheek again, he gazed into the fogging mirror. Wiping the condensation away with his free hand, a shocking site appeared. "You!" he shouted, seeing the face of the drunk driver replace his own.

He drove his bladed fist into the glass, cracking it in two. A large shard broke off, shattering into the sink. Tim looked up again, hoping beyond all hope his enemy was still there. To his disappointment, only *he* remained.

Dropping the razor, Tim walked away. Something was very wrong. Having imagined hurting the drunk driver in his mind, it was the first time it spilled into reality. Dr. Abel couldn't escape the demon from his past. The truth was…he wasn't sure if he wanted to run away or towards it.

*****

Day turned to night. Tim Abel drove his BMW down a dark, desolate road. He was tired, having tended an overbooked load of patients that day. Though he wasn't headed home. Putting foot to gas, he sped towards the spot of his wife's death.

Knowing its exact location, he retraced her path every night. Her final flip was in the near distance, within eyesight. Suddenly, a bright pair of headlights blazed forward. In the opposite lane, Tim thought nothing of it. However, as the lights got brighter, he realized something.

"Is that car on the wrong side of the road? I think he's coming at me!"

The opposite car raced forward with blazing speed, faster than Dr. Abel could react. Tim jerked the wheel, attempting to avoid a head-on collision. However, the car swerved in his direction. It was clearly aiming for the doctor, hunting him down. Tim shouted in horror. Right before contact, the headlights faded. It was a souped-up Mazda, favored by drag racers.

It was the same exact car that hit his wife, head-on.

Tim gasped in disbelief, freezing in fear. He'd only seen the drunk's vehicle demolished in a junkyard. The doctor remembered seeing it compacted into scrap, regretting never destroying it himself.

However, it was suddenly whole again. The drunk's vehicle rammed into Tim's car, crushing every ounce of metal. Tim felt it smash every bone in his body, just like his wife felt. Though after the excruciating pain, he was denied the right to die, to join his love.

Skidding off road into a ditch, Dr. Abel gazed around. There was no other car in sight, no accident. Stepping out of the vehicle, he was in the exact spot his wife's car landed. He trembled, realizing, *I need help...damn it. I need it now!*

*****

Tim Abel entered a therapist's office. He sat in the cold waiting room, stiff and uncomfortable. Such a setting was not a norm for the man, as giving up control was unthinkable. His motto was, *Doctors don't go to doctors...no matter what type of doctor they are! Physical or mental health...I only trust my own knowledge of medicine. The others are a bunch of quacks.*

However, the darkness, which once burned his photo albums, grew darker. It neared unspeakable acts. He knew if something didn't change soon, he'd act upon them. Though as minutes ticked in the waiting room, fear of the unknown overtook him. *I'll take my chances on my own,* he thought, heading toward the door.

Another door opened, an attractive 40-year-old blond exited. "Mr. Abel?" she asked.

Without a thought, Tim corrected her. "*Doctor*...Abel," he said, stopping his flight. He turned to see the attractive woman.

Impressed by the man's powerful response, she momentarily felt like the one in a position of submission. That power quickly changed back again. She extended a friendly hand, "I'm Dr. Shelly Cole."

Tim accepted Shelly's greeting. The look of surprise was on his face. He didn't expect to feel a bold grip, matching his own. "Hello," he said coldly and untrusting. "I was under the belief...you were a man."

"What gave you that impression?"

He paused in thought. "I just saw Dr. Cole...not your first name."

"Is that an issue for you? I can refer you to a fellow male colleague...if it makes you more comfortable."

"No...I'm not a misogynist...if that's what you're implying."

"Relax, Dr. Abel...I'd never say such a thing," she assured.

"But you're thinking it," he said in an insulted tone.

"Did you come to discuss my issues...or yours?"

He exhaled, "Sorry."

"No reason to apologize, doctor. You were just speaking your thoughts...something I encourage. Now tell me...why were you leaving? Did you not like my magazine selection?" she asked, smiling.

"I...think this was a mistake."

"We haven't even started yet...how do you know?"

"I just know," he declared.

"Tell me doctor, what if one of your patients walked out before you could treat them? Would they be better off giving in to fear...or worse?"

"I'm not afraid!" he proclaimed.

"Then come inside...give me a chance."

"Fine," he said, puffing his alpha chest. The 54-year-old man strutted toward Dr. Shelly Cole's office.

*****

Shelly shut the door, seeing Tim Abel studying her many diplomas on the wall. "Do I make the credential cut?"

"Just seeing where you went to school...that's all."

"I was just teasing, doctor. Take a seat," she said, studying his nervous body language. Waiting for him to sit on the couch, she followed in her leather chair. "Tell me why you're here today."

He exhaled again, pausing before his response. "Well to start...I'm seeing things."

"What kind of things? Ghosts?"

"I don't believe in ghosts, Dr. Cole. I'm not a nutcase...don't treat me like one."

"I apologize if I offended you, but you have to work with me."

"Fine. It's a man."

"Someone you know? A stranger?"

"Both."

"Can you elaborate a little more?"

"He's a stranger that I know."

"OK. How do you know him? Is he an estranged friend?"

"He's no friend of mine. In fact...he's a mortal enemy."

"So he's caused you past grief."

"Yes."

"Have there been any recent events to trigger such visions?"

"No. I mean…he's always on my mind. And to be honest, dark thoughts always follow him. Though now…they've reached a level of obsession which is unhealthy. No, worse than that…dangerous."

"Dangerous? To whom?"

"Myself…others."

"Elaborate. Who else are they dangerous to?"

He paused again, "I don't feel comfortable saying."

"Fair enough," Dr. Shelly Cole said. "Perhaps in time, when I've earned your trust, you'll feel more comfortable."

"Perhaps," he said, rolling his eyes in disbelief.

"Then lets start with something you're comfortable with. Tell me about your life, your family."

"I'm a doctor…my son, Sean is a doctor, and my daughter, Darcy, just graduated high-school. She's my stepdaughter, to be exact, though she's family to me. They both just got married."

"Congratulations. Do you approve of their choice in spouses?"

Tim paused again. "I do…since they're married to each other."

The therapist was the one pausing next. However, after calculating the facts, she smiled, "Very nice."

"I know…you think they'll have a three-headed child."

Shelly's face cringed, as she thought, *How'd he know I was thinking that?* "Never!" she exclaimed. "It's not like they're related by blood. Besides…I'm not here to judge you, doctor. I'm here to help you…I'm your ally."

"For what I'm paying you…you better be."

She smiled again. He paused, staring deeply at her expression. A glimmer shined in his eyes, one that hadn't shined in years. However, it quickly turned to sadness.

"Is something wrong?" she asked.

"No, why?"

"The expression on your face...it was one of sad reflection."

"My wife...*your* smile...reminded me of my wife's," he said in pain.

"Is that not a good thing?" she asked.

"My wife passed away," he said in heartache.

A look of hurt crossed Shelly Cole's face. It was deeper than sympathy, closer to empathy. "I'm so sorry to hear that," she said, rising from her chair to hug the man. The hug was warm, sincere, and heartfelt.

Slow to return the hug, Tim thought, *Why not?* He returned the offering, placing his arms around her curvy body. Her long blond hair draped over his face. A pheromone struck his nose. She was rose-petal scented like his deceased-wife. It wasn't the only fact to awaken his senses.

It was the care in her touch, rubbing his strong back in support. His hands returned the rub, slowly slipping downward. In near trance, his fingers traced her waist, riding the curves of her hips. He slid downward. Reading her like Braille, Shelly was like a roadmap to his past. She was like his wife.

"Excuse me, doctor...can you remove your hands from my...behind?"

A gasp exited Tim Abel's mouth, as he quickly removed his grasp. "I'm so sorry, you must believe me. I didn't mean to do that...you just felt like...*her*. It's just been so long..."

"It's completely fine, doctor...and normal."

"It is?"

"Yes. Transference. Because I asked you to remember her...your feelings temporarily transfer to me. It passes quickly, nothing to worry about."

He shook his head in agreement, even though he knew better. He'd hugged other women since losing his wife, though none of them caused *that* reaction. "Right."

"Tell me about her."

"Debra Smith...the most beautiful blond hair I've ever seen. Eyes as blue as the ocean. Not the Atlantic. More like the Caribbean. Her body...my God! Curves you could sled on for miles. Her hair smelled like roses, skin too."

Shelly saw the love in the man's eyes, pain equaling it. The tone of his voice was passion, a contrast from the stiff man who arrived there. Shelly found herself lost in his words, his voice. Having seen many patients speak of loss and love, no one had affected her in the same way. The realization spooked her.

"You obviously loved her, do you mind telling me how you lost her?"

Tim's face turned from light to darkness. "It was a dark night, rainy. She was driving home from work, a desolate road. Her last words to me were emailed...*I love you.* I always told her I thought technology was robbing our humanity. I'd give anything to tell her directly, hear her voice...one last time. I didn't get *that* opportunity."

"She got into a car accident?"

Tim's face grew cold, angry. "She was murdered."

Shelly Cole's face turned pale. "I'm so sorry to hear that. Was the killer caught?"

"Oh he was caught alright...a month in jail...and a letter of apology to me."

"I never heard of such a light sentence for murder! Did you write him back?"

"I wrote him...though never sent it. I couldn't find the words. There just weren't enough *fuck you's* I could fit on the page to do my anger justice. He was a drunk driver."

A loud gasp sounded from the therapist's mouth. The unorthodox act was not usual for her. However, chills crossed her skin. Dark memories clouded her own mind. "I...don't know what to say..."

Dr. Abel said, "It's OK. It's been ten years now...yet I still can't adequately explain it. It still feels like yesterday. A 24-year-old punk...beer cans filled the floorboards. He had a fresh 12-pack in the passenger seat, a bottle in his hand. Add to that...the fucker was texting. He hit her head-on...totaled both vehicles. My wife was crushed, dead at the scene. The kid...barely a scratch."

A sick look covered Dr. Shelly Cole's face. Her trembling leg jittered the oak floor. She wanted to share her own pain with him, though knew her job was to help him, not visa-versa. "I don't have the words to heal such a tragedy."

"I didn't expect you to. I guess...I just hoped you'd point me in the direction of sanity...before I lose my mind."

Needing to change the subject, she asked, "In all this time...no romance?"

"Nothing worth keeping."

"Let me guess...no one compares?"

"No one *I've* met."

She nodded. "You mentioned a stepdaughter...I'm assuming that was Darcy's mother."

"It was."

"How's her development been?"

"Great. She's a full C-cup now."

"I meant...mental development, doctor."

"Right. My mind has a direction of its own..."

"You're a man, it's expected. Go on."

"She's grown into an amazing person."

"It's good to see the past hasn't stopped her from love."

"She doesn't know."

"About what?"

"The drunk driver."

"Why not?"

"Why hurt her?" he asked. "As you said...she turned out fine."

"Maybe it's time to tell her the truth. More relevant to our purposes here...maybe it's time you spoke the truth."

"I don't understand."

"You've carried this painful secret around...shouldering all the burden yourself...and you wonder why you can't move on?"

"I do it for my stepdaughter...I do it for Darcy!"

"I wonder about *that*."

"Are you calling me a liar?"

"No, doctor...I'm calling you a survivor. Darcy's not the only one you're protecting."

"Then who else?"

"Yourself," she declared.

He rose in anger, "How dare you suggest that! I'm not a selfish man...in fact, I gave up my fucking life to protect her from the pain."

"You did...you're a kind, great man. I could easily leave it there...but my job is to lay the truth out...no matter how much you don't care to hear it. You feared *dealing* with her pain...as much as *seeing* her in it. No one blames you for that."

"So what are you saying? I should tell her now? Then all my problems just suddenly vanish?"

"You're an educated man, Dr. Abel. You know it's much more complicated than that. However...it'll be a start. It's time to travel the road to recovery."

"I can't do it."

"Why not?"

"She'll hate me...for hiding it."

"You're afraid."

"I told you before entering...I'm not afraid!"

"You are! You fear letting go. You fear feeling better. Most of all, you fear being pain-free. You've worn hurt like a cloak, and you fear what's to come. You fear what will happen when you look around and realize you've wasted half your life alone...chasing ghosts!'"

Shock filled him, wondering how the therapist could've known his personal pain so well. However, he reacted in vulnerable anger. "Bullshit!" he shouted, rushing for the exit.

"I'm sorry for my tone, Dr. Abel. I just want you to give yourself a chance at life! It's waiting for you!"

He exited. Shelly exhaled, sad to see him go. Though, she was sad for another reason as well. The therapist's wise advice was something she couldn't follow herself.

CHAPTER TWO

Two Months Later

"I'm so sorry, Sean," Darcy pleaded.

"I'm not blaming you...we don't know who's at fault," Sean said in a stressed voice.

"My mother always said fertile women run in the family. We were made to be knocked-up."

"So it's *you* putting the blame on *me*! You think I'm not man enough...that I'm shooting blanks?"

"No, that's not what I mean...well, kinda...but not in a bad way."

"Then you're insulting my manhood in a...*good way?*"

"Not at all, baby. I just don't know what to do. It's been two months, and nothing's happened. Can we see someone?" she asked timidly, knowing Sean hated other doctors.

"No!" he exclaimed.

"But why not?"

"We'll just keep trying until it happens."

"I don't wanna be one of those sad couples...waiting forever to get pregnant. I don't wanna see all my friends pushing babies in strollers, on swings, wishing I was them."

Sean exhaled in stress. "I know, I know. I just...don't want to..."

"Don't want to what? What are you afraid of, Sean?"

"I don't fear anything!"

"You're just like stepdad! Why can't men just admit when they're scared?"

"Fine, you wanna know what scares the living shit out of me? Watching my manhood die before my eyes! That's what scares me, Darcy!"

Darcy put her arms around him. "You're still *my* man, no matter what! Am I any less of a woman if it's my fault?"

"The expectations are different for men. You just don't understand. It's my job to impregnate you, my job to produce offspring. The need's as old as cavemen themselves!"

"Who cares what anyone thinks? Just like our relationship...we didn't get anyone's permission. We did it *our* way."

"I care what *I* think...and it would make *me* a failure. Besides, I don't trust any of these wackos with the results. Half of these OBGYN's are high on narcotics."

Nervousness filled Darcy, fearful to make her suggestion. However, she thought, *What do I have to lose at this point? Screw it, just say it!* "Well...there's always *stepdad*," she said, cringing.

"You can't be serious," Sean accused.

"Just think about it...he's already seen me...*naked*," she looked down, averting her eyes from her stepbrother husband. "And he's so smart! You know you can trust what he says."

Sean knew Darcy was correct. He admired his OBGYN father's knowledge, though he couldn't imagine the man intimately examining Darcy again. However, he also wanted to make her happy. Few things were more important than the alpha-doctor's pride, though his step-wife's joy was one of them. "For you...I'll do it."

Tears entered Darcy's eyes. She kissed his lips. "Thank you, baby. I promise, no matter how it goes, I'll love you until the day I die. You'll always be my man, always!"

He nodded, fear still gleaming in his eyes. Although he didn't say it, his pained inner-thoughts spoke louder than words. *I just hope I can live with the results.*

*****

"Welcome," Tim Abel greeted, entering his exam room.

Darcy was in her medical gown, sitting nervously in the gyno chair. *Me and my big mouthed stupid ideas! Stepdad examining me for infertility while stepbrother husband watches! What was I thinking? Sean will end up killing his own father over jealousy!*

Sean Abel was uncomfortable, never-before entering the family medical practice as a patient. Taking one gaze at the gyno chair, his skin crawled. Seeing the look on his son's face, Tim Abel reached into a drawer, removing a white coat from within. Handing the spare to Sean, he said, "Take the edge off, doctor."

Sean nodded, "Thanks," he said, putting it on. He still felt strange, though like a frightened child with his favorite blanket, it brought a sense of comfort. Unfortunately, *that* security soon faded.

Dr. Tim Abel handed his son a plastic cup. "Go into the bathroom and ejaculate into the sterile cup. We have visual stimulation...magazines...videos...if needed..."

"I know, dad...I work here too."

"I'm just being official," Tim informed his son.

Sean grabbed the cup in humiliation. He headed into the sample room, as Tim approached Darcy in the gyno chair. Both of them looked awkward, remembering the last time they were in the exam room. Orally and anally stimulated by her step-doctor, the redhead felt like she was living it again. As much as she wanted to deny it, the situation turned her on.

Dr. Tim Abel ordered the curvy patient, "Place your feet in the stirrups." Darcy complied, exposing her wet snatch. After snapping on latex gloves, Tim stepped between his stepdaughter's spread legs.

His mouth watered from the scent of her arousal. The sight of her pink pussy made him rock-hard. Although he no longer had romantic love for Darcy, he couldn't deny the physical pleasure he got from anally conquering her.

"Before I start, I need to ask you a few questions. Sean too."

"Can I take my legs down, cover up during it?"

"No," he said, failing to give a reason.

"OK, doctor...stepdad," she said submissively.

The door opened, as a white-coated Sean slowly walked out. He was red from both strain and embarrassment. "Here," he said, holding the cum-filled cup in his hands. Unable to look his father in the eye, he stared downward.

Unhindered by such situations, the senior doctor took the cup without pause. Pulling out a black marker, he wrote the name Abel on it, putting it aside. Darcy focused on the cup, thinking, *Wow, that's one big load. Could he actually be turned on by this...or was it the porn mags? Probably the porn.*

"Take a seat, Sean."

"I'd rather stand," he said, not wanting to feel like a patient.

"No problem," Tim responded. "First, I want to say...in most cases, we prefer to wait 12 months to officially diagnose infertility. Are you sure you don't want to wait and see if it happens naturally?"

"No," Darcy chimed in. "I want it now."

"OK, onto the first question. *Family history.* Well...no need for that." Tim checked the box. "Did your last partner, predating your spouse, have any type of sexually transmitted diseases? Actually, lets skip that one as well." Knowing that Darcy's last partner was the doctor himself, they all appreciated the omission. "In fact...let's just move on to the examination," Tim said.

"Good idea," Sean agreed.

"Can I go pee now? You told me to drink all this water...I think I'm gonna burst."

"We'll get to that soon enough, Darcy," the step-doctor assured.

Stepping in-between the redheaded patient's legs, his hunger for her grew. Sean quickly joined him, both men crowded for a spot. Darcy's heart thumped hard. She stared at her stepfather and stepbrother lodged between her spread thighs.

Dr. Tim Abel announced, "I'm going to perform a series of tests. Since the man's responsible for 30% of infertility cases, women 70%, Darcy's tests will be a bit more...invasive. We'll start with a transvaginal ultrasound."

"This probably won't work on me...since I'm not a transvestite. Can we just move on to the next test?" Darcy asked.

"Nice try," Tim responded.

"Ultra...*sound*...so you'll be looking in my ears, right? Testing my hearing?" Darcy asked in hope, even though she knew better.

"Wrong end," Tim announced. "This *sound...*is in your vagina. Sound waves, of course."

Dr. Tim Abel unveiled a thick 4-inch probe. It was attached by wire to a computer monitor. Thicker than the usual transvaginal probe, it stimulated the patient to get more accurate results. He added a disposable sheath over the plastic wand.

The doctor activated the monitor screen. He added ultrasound gel to the probe's end, spreading Darcy with latex fingers. Then he slowly slid it into her moist mound. She moaned, legs stiffened, feet dug into steel stirrups. The probe went from thinner to widest at the base. With every inch, Darcy was stretched open further

It seemed unending, pressing her full bladder from the inside. Multiple sensations struck her, ranging from a urination sting to pained insertion to sexual heat. She couldn't figure out which one would win out. She silently thought, *I will not cum! It was bad enough doing that in front of each step-doctor separately! I can only imagine how embarrassing it would be together! Uh!*

The feeling only got worse as Dr. Tim Abel pressed upward on the probe. Feeling her G-spot squashed, Darcy imagined herself leaping from the gyno chair, head stuck in ceiling. Orgasm was creeping closer, her fluids spilling like nectar of the gods.

Dr. Tim Abel activated the probe. Sound waves sailed through Darcy's vaginal velvet, a black and white image appeared on the monitor. The ovaries and uterus were on screen. Tim moved it around fast and roughly, up and down, side to side. "Oh-ly crapola!" she shouted, tensing hard.

"Try not to tense," Stepfather Abel instructed.

Not hearing a word he said, Darcy's kegel muscles contracted. Choking the slick and slippery wand with her pussy, her sexual nerves were ablaze with fire. Each probing struck a different part of her. The most painfully stimulating was the G-spot gland. Trying to hold her urine in, Darcy's tightening canal burned with greater sexual flames.

While the two step-doctors watched the monitor screen, sweat beaded down Darcy's forehead. Her breath huffed, heart raced. The curvy redhead bit her bottom lip to a bleeding point. Grasping the chair rails, she silently begged herself, *Don't cum...please...don't do it!*

The slick probe sailed back, forth, up, down, left, right. "I'm cumming!" Darcy shouted, shocking the two doctors. They looked over, watching the redhead shake like a runaway washing machine. Her eyes rolled upward, teeth gnashed as one. Tim Abel kept the probe going, knowing better than to leave a patient aimlessly grinding.

Darcy's feet slipped from the stirrups, shutting her thighs, smashing the wand between them. She humiliatingly humped the thick invader, cumming upon the medical instrument. Pained pleasure reverberated through her curvy body, coating the plastic covering in feminine cream.

As she calmed, her worst fear was realized. *OMG! I orgasmed in front of my stepfather and stepbrother together. Husband or not...this was so embarrassing! Ooohhh...I really gotta pee!* "Can I go now? Like...as in...pee?"

"Absolutely," Dr. Tim Abel said.

Darcy quickly attempted to escape, Dr. Tim Abel stopped her from exiting. "Stay seated."

"Don't I get to use the porn bathroom too?" Darcy asked.

"No. I need to perform a luteinizing hormone test, checking to see if you're ovulating properly. I'll need two separate fresh, sterile samples. I'll switch containers mid-stream," he said to both his son and stepdaughter's shock. Sean never took samples like that. Taking the cup in hand, Tim pressed on Darcy's abdomen. Locating the bladder, he pressed hard, forcing the curvy redhead to urinate.

Darcy's face turned fire red. Her body tightened and tensed. She already had to pee before arriving, though the latex press made it intensely worse. The more Darcy fought it, the more pressure her stepfather applied. Slight moans sounded from the curvy redhead.

Gazing over at her stepbrother husband, Darcy hoped he'd step in. He did exactly that. To her surprise, it wasn't to stop it, but join in. Sean thought, *If I can't beat him, I'll join him damn it!* Slapping on a pair of latex gloves, both of Sean Abel's hands pressed upon his stepsister wife's bladder.

Tim proudly smiled, happy to work in tandem with his son. In their time working together, it was a first. Suddenly, Darcy's loud gasp filled the room. Leaving Sean to press, Dr. Tim Abel grabbed two specimen cups. He held a plastic cup in each hand, placing one at the base of his stepdaughter's ass. After more intense pressing, Darcy's hard fought battle for urination was finally lost. She was forced to let go, letting a stream sail from her inner depths.

One step-doctor kept pressure on her abdomen, keeping his wife flowing, the other spread her wide, collecting her offering. Darcy froze in forced submission. *I'm peeing in front of my stepfather and stepbrother...holy hell...someone shoot me now!*

With no other option, she kept filling the specimen cup. The longer it took to empty her bladder, the more humiliated she became. Though her stiffened nipples told a different story. As much as she didn't want to admit it, the voyeuristic show turned her on. Being watched by the two step-doctors simultaneously, aroused her beyond words.

In mid-stream, Tim switched cups. "Just keep going, don't stop," he instructed.

As the last trickle landed, Dr. Tim Abel capped and labeled both specimen cups. Sean Abel wiped Darcy with a disinfectant pad, making his step-sister wife sting with pleasure.

Both step-doctors remained between Darcy's thighs. Tim lubed his co-doctor's finger with a squirt. The surprised 30-year-old gladly accepted. "We'll perform a duel digital exam," Tim said proudly.

"You want my...assistance? Really, dad?"

"I'd be honored to have your help, son."

Darcy's mouth dropped open. *Are they really gonna finger me...together? Oh shit...this is nuts...and hot! And dangerous! Could I cum again? I've had multiples before. Shit!*

The two men entered their fingers into the sopping pink slit. Each one pushed forward, slowly. Tim examined one silky side, Sean the other. Stepfather and stepbrother sank deeper into Darcy's creamy cavern. Reaching their latex knuckles, they spun their fingers in circles.

They stretched their curvy young patient wide. Each one touched her G-spot, pressing upward, making Darcy squirm more. The deeper they moved inside her, the hotter each sexual nerve fired up. Wetness trickled from her pussy; orgasm wasn't far behind it.

Both men removed their fingers from the juicy fruit. They touched their index fingers to thumb, pulling sticky fluid apart. A cloudy string appeared. "Looks normal to me," Sean said.

"A normal sign of arousal," Tim said, making both Darcy and Sean blush.

Next, the doctor revealed a speculum. Spreading his stepdaughter wide, he slipped it inside her pink paradise. Clicking the metal medical tool, he stretched Darcy open. More evidence of a whitish wonderland showed itself, cloudy streams of quim awaited.

Grabbing a bristle brush, Dr. Tim Abel swabbed the vaginal cells in swirls. Darcy squirmed, though didn't cum again. However, the most involved exam had yet to begin. For the last act, the senior doctor grabbed a thin, flexible tube with a small, lighted camera on its end. Between the prior lubing and Darcy's natural wetness, he didn't need another.

The doctor attached the medical contraption to the monitor, activating it again. Not knowing what to expect, the curvy redhead tensed in nervousness. Still spread by the speculum, she couldn't stop the tube from entering her slippery slit.

Darcy was fine until it hit her cervical ring. She squirmed, reaching downward to pull it out. Tim ordered, "Hold her down, Sean!"

The strong stepbrother pinned his stepsister down, exposing her breasts in the struggle. Darcy removed her legs from the stirrups, kicking at her stepfather doctor, trying to stop him from entering her womb.

With no other choice, Tim Abel went for plan B. Having dealt with manically panicking patients before, a sleepy injection was the answer. The senior doctor readied an IV. "Tape her hand to the chair, we need to keep her steady for the needle!" Stepfather Tim ordered his son.

As bad as he felt, Sean knew it was for his wife's own good. Grabbing the medical tape, he secured his stepsister's arms to the handrails, wrists up.

"Sean...don't do this. I don't want a shot!" Darcy begged.

"Relax, baby...it's just twilight," he said, swabbing her soft skin at the inner elbow area. "You'll feel it less...fight it less."

Darcy's stepfather administered the needle, watching his mostly nude, curvy stepdaughter squirm more. He opened the IV, letting the liquid sedative flow. The fight calmed, her body capitulated to her step-doctors. Darcy's eyes got heavy, stepbrother's gloved fingers slipped through red hair, comforting her into a heavy daze.

The patient went limp in the gyno chair. Dr. Tim Abel placed Darcy's feet back in the stirrups. Sean taped them into place, spreading his unconscious stepsister wide. Tim guided the tube deeper inside, threading the exploratory camera through the cervical ring. Looking at the monitor's screen, Dr. Abel snaked the camera throughout her womb. He examined each ovary closely, ensuring their full health.

In the midst of his exam, his son further exposed Darcy's breasts. Sean groped them roughly. Seeing his father's stare, Sean said, "I figured...a breast exam couldn't hurt."

Tim nodded, "Good idea. In fact..." Tim said, placing his finger against Darcy's asshole, he pressed inward to the sleepy sphincter. "I think a rectal exam is in order as well."

Darcy gently moaned, feeling multiple sensations fill her. It felt like a dream, like her fantasy, being examined by her stepfather and stepbrother simultaneously. Tim Abel pushed deeper into her womanhood, exploring every inch. He also swirled his finger inside her anal wonderland, checking her rectum.

Pressing a button, Dr. Tim Abel released a biopsy needle from the inner tube. A tissue sample was collected from the uterus. Pleasure and pain buzzed Darcy's hazy mind. Her body ached to cum again, fighting sleep itself to do so. She could feel her stepbrother pinching her nipples, roughly squeezing her breasts. At the same moment, she felt her stepfather's tools invade her ass and pussy. However, she could only enjoy it in theory, as exhaustion captured her.

Though Darcy couldn't fully appreciate the moment, Sean Abel did. As much as it made him jealous, watching his stepfather command his wife brought unexpected comfort. *I trust my father to do what's right...for the both of us. She's in good hands...and I have no doubt that by the end of this...she'll be pregnant.*

✳✳✳✳✳

"Mr. Abel?" Dr. Shelly Cole asked in shock. She was headed home for the night.

"Miss Cole...I mean, Dr. Cole, I'm sorry to surprise you like this...I know I don't have an appointment. I see you're leaving...I'll come back another time," he said, quickly turning for the exit.

"Doctor...stop," she demanded.

Tim Abel was not used to orders, yet he obeyed. Turning back to face her, he awaited her words.

"Come inside, please."

✳✳✳✳✳

Inside the office, the doctor was as uncomfortable as their first meeting, two months ago. He sat on the couch, wanting to run out.

Shelly Cole sat in her seat. "It's good to see you again, doctor."

"And you," he said in a stiff tone.

158

"It's been a while."

"It has."

"The last time we spoke, you mentioned a stepdaughter...Darcy, I believe," she said.

Tim's phone suddenly rang. It was a song called, *La Vie en Rose*, by Louis Armstrong. "Speaking of my stepdaughter...that's her ringtone. I'll call her back. And yes, she introduced me to ringtones. All this phone technology's foreign to me."

"Great song."

"Yeah, I call her my red rose...the song was fitting. You have a good memory...after all these months...and just one meeting."

"It's easy to remember when you care about people," she said sincerely. "I thought about you often these last two months. I was worried about you."

"Why me?"

She blushed, realizing she'd been too honest. "Uh...I worry about all my patients' well-being. But more specific to your case...my worry stemmed from your inner-anger...deeply harbored pain."

"Ah, so it's *myself* I need saving from. I'm beginning to recall why I ran out of here...haven't returned."

Dr. Cole smiled warmly, "Most of us are our own worst enemies, doctor."

"You included?"

Now Shelly Cole was the one to pause. She appeared apprehensive. "I'll play along. Sure, some times of my life...worse than others."

"Not nearly as dark as my situation."

"You shouldn't *assume*...as the saying goes...it makes an ass out of you and...well, *just* you. I'm sorry, that was unprofessional..."

"No, you're correct. How would I know your pain? Unless you're willing to tell me..."

"Doctor, this is your treatment, not mine."

"Right, sorry again. None of my business."

"It's fine...let's get back to you," she said, wearing an uncomfortable expression.

Tim Abel shifted in his chair, wishing Shelly Cole had taken the spotlight instead. Though more than that, he wanted to know about her. The look in her eyes was strangely familiar to him. He'd suddenly realized, it was the same pain which stared back in the mirror. "Go ahead, ask what you want to ask."

"Before I do...promise me something," she requested.

"Sure."

"Give me a chance. Don't run out on me...disappearing for two months. Don't quit before you've even begun. Allow me to help you, doctor...please, sir."

Tim Abel nodded. "You have my word."

"Thank you. We'll get back to Darcy in a moment...but first, I'd like to discuss the visions from last session."

"Wow, you *really* have a good memory. I still see him...more often with each day. I see the drunk driver so much...he's become normal to me."

"The dark thoughts still there?"

"Darker than ever."

"Are you ready to talk about it...tell me what those thoughts are?"

He exhaled, stress plastered his face. "I am."

"Were they thoughts of self-harm?"

"At one point, yes. Though, those days have long passed."

"Thoughts of harming others?"

Dr. Abel turned pale, gulping. *Should I dare tell her? She can have me arrested...doctor-patient confidentiality is easily broken. Though it's that look in her eyes...it's like, she knows...feels my pain. I think I can trust her...I think I can take the risk.* The look on his face answered for him. "Just one."

Strangely, Shelly Cole didn't look surprised. "You don't have to tell me who...but can you please tell me why?"

"Mike Robertson."

"Who is he to you?"

"A name I'll never forget. A man...no, he's not a man. The scum I'll curse until the day I die. He's the devil of my world."

"Explain."

"He murdered my wife!" Tim Abel shouted angrily.

"I'm sorry, doctor. I know how hard it is to speak his name. Though, is harming him the answer?"

"Aren't you supposed to tell me that?"

She paused, as if she was hoping to hear it herself. Then, she remembered to recite the responsible thing. "Of course, it's always wrong to harm anyone..."

"No, it's wrong to harm the *innocent*. It's wrong to get behind the wheel of a *car*...to drive into someone head-on! It's NOT wrong to take an axe to that scumbag's head...to burn him alive. Or eye for an eye...drive him right into a brick wall!" he shouted at the top of his lungs. The normally composed man was beet red, trembling. He nearly foamed at the mouth with rabidity.

Shelly's heart pounded, fist clenched. She wanted nothing more than to scream, *Do it! Do it now...for me!* Of course, she took an oath against such advice. "Relax, doctor! I shouldn't have to school you in the dangers of raised blood pressure! You'll be the one to die, if you don't take a breath!"

Hearing her words, the doctor sat back down. He grasped his salt and pepper hair in frustration. Wheeling her chair closer to Tim, Shelly placed her hand on his knee. Her mere touch calmed the doctor like only one other had: his deceased wife.

"Your kids...think about them. They don't want to lose their father...have him sent to jail."

"I don't plan on going to jail."

"Such a crime leaves evidence behind...things you can't anticipate, clues to your identity you'll never realize exist!"

"Good point," Tim said, thinking, *It almost sounds like she's considered killing before.* After taking another look at her feminine curvy frame, he thought, *Not a chance.*

"Let's not speak of such pain...let's talk about good things. Darcy. Tell me about her."

"She's an amazing girl. Just turned 19."

"You really care for her. I see it in your eyes."

"I do. When she lost her mother...she became my world. I wanted to save her, protect her..."

"And you did that."

"I tried."

"It sounds like you did a fine job of raising her."

"I wasn't perfect."

"No one is."

"No...I did a terrible thing. In giving everything to protect her, I abandoned my son in the process."

"I'm sure he forgives you."

"He does...though it's myself I can't forgive."

"And this brings us back to my point...the one I made two months ago. Doctor, your son wasn't the only one you abandoned that day. You abandoned yourself as well...abandoned life itself."

Another deep exhale exited Tim Abel's mouth. It was like he finally capitulated his denial. He was too exhausted to fight anymore. "You're right."

"It's time to lift your burden. It's time to tell Darcy the truth. She deserves to know how her mother died, and you deserve to release this secret you've carried around all these years. I know you think avoiding truth helped you both...but it hasn't."

"She'll never forgive me for lying."

"You didn't lie...you just didn't tell. If Darcy's the loving girl you describe, she'll understand...I promise."

After a long pause, a look of resolution crossed Tim Abel's face. "Can that really free all the pain?"

"I don't know, doctor. Every person processes pain and release different. But I do know it's worth the shot."

"OK, Dr. Cole. For you...I'll do it."

"No, Dr. Abel. Do this for you. It's time to start healing."

CHAPTER THREE

"Welcome back," Dr. Tim Abel greeted his son and stepdaughter.

They flashed nervous smiles at him, unsure of what was to come. The prior appointment was interesting to say the least. "Hi, stepdad," Darcy said. "I think I'm ovulating...as you asked."

"Great...I'll just check to make sure. It's important for today's exam."

"Father," Sean Abel said, nodding hello. "Can you loan me a medical coat again?"

"I don't believe you'll need it, son."

"Why's that?" Sean asked suspiciously.

"Because this particular exam doesn't require clothes."

"For Darcy," Sean stated.

"For both," Dr. Tim Abel informed.

Both their faces turned to shock. Darcy said, "Umm...total nakedness?"

"Yes," Tim declared.

"Dad, I'm a doctor. There's no exam I know of requiring a couple to be naked."

"Correct, son. A General Practitioner wouldn't be familiar with it, but an OBGYN would."

"Don't forget the T, step-dad."

Sean looked at her with a crazy gaze. "T?"

"OBGYN and T...for throat," she said.

Sean looked at his stepfather in an even more confused manner. Dr. Tim Abel said, "It's a specialty I studied in my spare time. Never mind that...we must solve this infertility problem! The exam is called a post coital test."

"Wait a minute! Post as in *after*...coital as in *sex*?" Sean asked in disbelief.

"Relax, son. I won't be present during the act."

"Since when is sex sanctioned in a medical setting?" Sean questioned.

"It's often not...the couple usually returns home for a few hours. Unfortunately, they often return too late. The results get skewed. I won't risk that with my son and stepdaughter. You have my word. By the end of our time together...Darcy will carry the Abel seed...no matter what I have to do to achieve it."

"So we'll get it on...in here?" Darcy asked.

"I'll move you to one of the more comfortable rooms. One with a plush medical table."

"Tell me what happens...*post*...sex," Sean demanded.

"I'll examine Darcy...test the sperms survival rate time. Plus check the acidity of her cervical mucus. It's a very important test to administer."

The couple's hearts pounded in unison, as they knew it had to be done. They nodded, both remaining silent.

*****

Entering the room, Dr. Tim Abel walked them in. Sean exhaled, thinking, *I've had sex in here before...though as a doctor. There's something about being a patient that sickens me. It's like my power's been stripped away, like I've been neutered! Instead of feeling horny, I feel nauseous. This isn't a good start. Can I even get it up? Shit, why'd I even think that? The thought alone will cause it!*

Tim entered, handing Sean a white medical coat. "Your requested coat," Tim said.

The 30-year-old doctor paused, staring at it. He set it aside. "At the moment, I just don't feel very doctor-like," Sean said.

Dr. Tim Abel nodded, approaching Darcy. He revealed a long thermometer. "I'll need you to remove your pants and underwear, Mrs. Abel," Tim said in his professional voice.

"I thought you were leaving us alone in here?" Sean asked in a stressed voice.

"This is just to assure ovulation," Tim said. "As you know...a rise in body temperature is always a sign of it."

Darcy exhaled deeply, obeying her stepfather. Removing her shoes and socks, her cute feet were unveiled. She unbuttoned her jeans, dropping them to her ankles, kicking them away. Pausing with hands on her white panties, she stared up at her entranced stepfather and stepbrother. While Sean had a stressed gaze upon him, Tim Abel was visibly hard with lust.

The redhead pulled down her underwear. Her red pubic hair had grown back since her last shaving. Sean wanted to see the flaming beauty contrast against her pale pussy again.

Having not seen such a site, Darcy's stepfather got even more erect. "I need you to lie on the table," he said, patting the paper-lined surface. She approached him, as he lifted her up to the flat bed. Lying flat, her heart beat faster. "Spread your legs," her stepfather ordered.

Obeying the step-doctor, her thighs parted. She could feel her stepbrother's eyes burning, seething with jealousy. However, her thoughts were quickly removed from him. Tim Abel spread the wet, pink lips further apart. Darcy gasped, feeling the cold glass thermometer enter her.

It sank deeper, nearly swallowed by her creamy canal. Stepfather Tim shut Darcy's legs, locking the probe tightly inside her. She wiggled, feeling the glass poke at her cervix. Tim Abel kept his latex hand on her soft thigh, arousing the curvy redhead. Gazing at her stepbrother, she saw his discomfort grow.

The longer it stayed inside her, the wetter she got. Darcy's thighs were spread again, the thermometer removed. Her humiliation rose as her stepfather grabbed a rag, saying, "There's sexual discharge blocking the gauge...I'll just clean it off..."

"That happens a lot, right stepdad?" Darcy asked.

"Not really," Tim Abel said, making the couple cringe in further embarrassment.

"99.6. You're correct...ovulation is occurring," Tim confirmed. "I'll leave you two love birds to enjoy each other. Take your time...no rush."

Tim Abel exited the room, as Darcy and Sean stared at each other. "Let's get this over with," Sean said, having no intentions of making love. He kicked off his shoes and socks, dropped his slacks and boxers in one shot. Like Darcy, he left his shirt on. He stroked his flaccid cock, trying to quickly get a rise. It wasn't cooperating.

"Maybe this will help," Darcy said, removing her shirt. Her bra came off, revealing perky C-cups. Sean's curvy stepsister-wife lie naked on the medical table. The muscular doctor felt his cock rise again. Darcy asked, "The doctor coat? For old time's sake," she winked.

He flung off his shirt, revealing a muscular body. After putting on the coat, he quickly leapt up on the medical table, knowing his erection might not last long. As he placed his cock head to Darcy's slit, he heard his head nurse's voice outside the door. Then he heard his father talking, "They're trying to conceive. Who knows, it may even be happening as we speak."

All the pressure and shame struck Dr. Sean Abel again. His mind returned to the submissive patient, at the mercy of his own father. Right before he could penetrate her, he went soft again. "Fuck!" he shouted.

"It's OK, baby," Darcy said, kissing him. "It's cold in here...it's like when we had sex in the pool, you shrank."

"This is different...I just...can't do it."

"What can we do? We need this...for a baby," she said sadly.

Stepping down from the table, Sean put on his pants. Leaving his white coat on, a muscular chest peeked out the slit. He exited the room, joining his father and blond head nurse. His sexy feminine colleague let out an impressed gasp, having never seen her boss so exposed. She quickly turned away in bashfulness.

"Dad...we need to talk," Sean said stiffly.

"Sure," Tim Abel said, joining his son. The head nurse walked away.

Sean whispered, "I...can't...*you know*."

"Ejaculate?"

"The cow before the milk," Sean cryptically hinted.

"You can't get erect?" Tim asked loudly.

A collective gasp sounded from everyone around. The staffs' gazes turned in Sean's direction.

"Shhhh! Dad, my employees just heard you say that! They'll never respect an impotent boss!"

"Oh don't be ridiculous...you hold their paychecks in your hands...they'll bow down in reverence. I can solve your problem."

"Viagra?"

"No, that chemical garbage alters your sperm."

"Then what?"

Dr. Tim Abel turned to Sean's head nurse. "Mia."

"Yes, doctor?" she asked.

"Your assistance is needed."

Oh shit! Sean thought silently. By the time he could protest, she was standing before both bosses. Tim Abel whispered quietly in her ear. She blushed ten shades deeper. "Yes, doctor," she said. Following instructions, she immediately went into the exam room.

"What did you tell her?" Sean asked.

"To help out."

"How?"

"Don't worry...it's an old-fashioned remedy. Works like a charm. It was standard practice when I started out. Just get in there and seed your stepsister...or wife."

Stressed beyond words, Sean let out another exhale. "Fuck it," he said, entering the room, slamming the door behind him.

Darcy was uncomfortable with the new female guest. "What's happening, Sean?" she asked.

"This is my head nurse, Darcy. Don't worry, she's just going to help...somehow."

Unable to look Sean in the eyes, head nurse Mia snapped on a pair of latex gloves. Doctor, please remove your pants."

Still unsure what was happening, Sean just wanted to get it over with. Removing his pants, his still flaccid cock appeared. He blushed as much as the nurse did, humiliated that his employee was seeing him exposed, far from his glory.

She bent down in front of him, grasping his cock with her latex palm. "First, I'm going to perform a milking of the penis," she said.

Darcy gasped, having never seen her step-husband touched by another woman. Sean tensed, feeling his sexy blond nurse stroking his manhood. With each masturbating motion, the strong doctor began to grow. He looked up at his curvy redheaded stepsister. Her nipples were swollen and pointed toward the heavens. The scent of her feminine arousal filled the room. Shame masked Darcy's face for feeling such pleasure.

Before he knew it, Sean Abel's cock reached its 7-inch max. His veins swelled, cock throbbed. Head nurse Mia could already see a clear glob of precum seeping from the man-slit. "I think I'm there," he announced. "You can stop now."

"Right...sorry," Mia said in disappointment, releasing her cock-hold. "Please lie on top of your wife...assume missionary position."

OK, I feel like I'm in science class! So mechanical! This sucks! Darcy thought.

Keeping his white coat on, the muscular doctor mounted his stepsister. He positioned himself between her legs. Placing his cock at Darcy's dripping snatch, he awaited his head nurse's action. He began shrinking again, informing the nurse, "My problem is *staying* hard...oh damn that's cold..." he shouted, feeling an unexpected glob of lube part his muscular ass cheeks.

The blond nurse's latex finger touched Sean's asshole, "I need you to bear down, boss," she said.

"Why?" he asked.

"I'm going to massage your prostate to keep you erect," she said, pushing hard into his tight sphincter.

Sean grunted, his strong body pressed into Darcy. The intense feeling made his cock even harder. He plunged into his wife. His newly stiffened spear disappeared into his stepsister's wet wonderland.

Darcy moaned loudly, penetrated without warning. Sean's cock invasion was quick and hard, stretching the pussy lips, snuggling inside velvet blankets. Her strong husband weighed down upon her, sweat rained.

The head nurse went knuckle deep, pressing downward on Sean's prostate. His bottom-up position allowed maximum pressure on the gland. Although the 30-year-old doctor had a prostate exam before, it was never in a sexual situation, nor by an attractive subordinate. With each new wiggling of the latex finger, Sean's cock grew longer, girth wider.

The curvy redhead moaned, feeling her husband bucking like a mad bull. A surge of sexual stamina filled Sean's body. His white coat draped them both, flying through the air like a cape. He pounded his stepsister-wife harder, crashing into her sopping wet pussy. Spits of sweet juice speckled his balls and thighs.

All the while, the blond nurse stimulated the swollen gland within. Placing a second finger at his asshole, she entered another. Sean grunted like a sexually enraged beast, crashing into Darcy like a runaway truck. The feeling was painful enough to make a man cry, pleasurable enough to make him beg.

Their sexy nurse stretched Sean's asshole, plunging into the sexual gland. Every nerve heated, the doctor's ass felt like it was on fire. Thick streams of clear fluid crept through his stiff shaft, spilling into Darcy.

The distinct heavy swell of sperm began its forward march. As humiliating as it was, neither Darcy nor Sean dared stop it.

Watching another woman manipulate her husband drove Darcy wild with jealous lust.

Sean continued pounding his stepsister, every muscle strained to a bulge. Thick arms stretched the medical coat, his tight ass connected to strong thighs and bulbous calves.

The blond nurse's fingers sank deeper inside her boss' ass. She pressed so hard Sean's prostate flattened. Beads of sweat poured from him, baptizing his stepsister in an erotic tempest. He crashed into Darcy so hard she shook with each landing.

Darcy thought, *Don't cum...this isn't for enjoyment! Oh shit, the more I tell myself not to...the more I wanna...CUM!* A high-pitched squeal filled the room, sailing through the whole building. Darcy's curvy body trembled in fits of hot passion. She'd never been fucked so aggressively. Her fire red hair dangled off the table, swaying like flickering flames.

Her stepbrother's cock was so deep it nearly broke through to her womb. She anxiously awaited his cum, hoping seed would finally take hold. Darcy's body tensed, toes grasped, feet spun around in crazed circles. Each of Sean's new thrusts got quicker, his strong chest chaffed his stepsister's stiff nipples.

Feeling Darcy's tender flesh choke his cock, he unleashed seed inside his stepsister. His shout was wolf-like, grainy, gristled and growly. Right as he came, the blond nurse pressed the hardest of all. A tidal wave flooded Darcy's pussy.

With each new spurt of semen, the blond milked his prostate harder. Just when he thought he couldn't fire another round, a new load was forced from inner depths. He just kept cumming, losing control of bodily functions. Shaking with sexual convulsions, he was hostage to latex fingers. He could've kept going all day, though was finally offered mercy as the head nurse withdrew from Sean's ass.

The doctor collapsed on his redheaded wife. The two sat there, reality suddenly taking hold again. As embarrassing as it all was, a greater thought overtook their minds.

Will we ever have a child...or was all this for nothing?

*****

"From the sound of things...I'd say it went well in there," Dr. Tim Abel said, returning to his exam room. Darcy nodded, waiting inside the gyno chair. She wore a gown, feet pressed into the stirrups. Sean was dressed, opting to keep the white coat on. He stood beside his stepsister-wife, looking down in embarrassment.

Tim Abel stepped between his stepdaughter's spread legs. To his disappointment, a large puddle of semen pooled on the chair, flooding the bottom of Darcy's ass cheeks. Snapping on a fresh pair of latex gloves, he entered the speculum inside the curvy redhead.

Already slick with shared love juice, he slid the metal beak contraption inside his patient. Clicking the lever, he forced Darcy's pink pussy open. She gasped with every further inch of gape. Once she was as wide as she'd go, Tim activated an internal speculum light.

Turning to his son, Dr. Tim Abel asked, "Would you like to assist me again?"

Knowing his sperm would be on display, a humiliated Sean said, "I'll sit this one out."

Tim nodded in understanding. Opening Darcy wider, the step-doctor took a look deep inside her. "We have a problem," he said in disappointment.

"I knew I was the fault! Just go ahead and shoot me now," Darcy said in sadness.

"Relax, Darcy," Stepfather Tim said. "It's nothing like that. It's just...you likely orgasmed extra hard, pushing downward."

Darcy blushed deeply red, "No comment."

The doctor continued. "Anyway...in the process...you ejected too much of his sperm for me to observe your bodily reaction."

"So we do it again?" Sean asked, tightening his ass cheeks.

"No," Tim informed. "I still have your sperm sample. Before you leave, I'll need you to fill another one."

"I can do that," Sean said in anal relief.

Dr. Tim Abel retrieved a sperm vial from the sample refrigerator. He took a rubber tipped syringe, sucking a large sample of sperm into its clear chamber. Once the test tube was empty, he headed back toward the patient.

Slipping the rubber tip into Darcy's tender tunnel, stepfather filled stepdaughter with stepbrother's sperm. He pressed down on the syringe's plunger, watching each cc disappear into Darcy's dripping snatch.

The curvy redhead tensed, trying not to get aroused by her stepbrother's cum coating her insides. A chilled heaviness filled her feminine depths. Just when she didn't think it could fill her more, another load invaded her speculum stretched pussy. Her body shook with lust; gown fell away at the breasts, revealing engorged nipples.

As the last cold shot of semen entered her, Tim Abel tilted the gyno chair. Aiming her butt upward, Darcy's head was lowered to the floor. "I added a little too much...so I'll let that drain for about ten minutes," the doctor said.

Tim sat. The three waited in silent awkwardness, male eyes fixated on Darcy. Her stirrup spread legs remained high in the air. A speculum stretched, cum-filled pussy was on display for their viewing.

After a long ten minutes, Dr. Abel returned Darcy to her seated position. "OK, now we'll need the excess semen to drain," Tim said. "I need you to push like you're going to the bathroom, help speed the emptying process along."

OMG! My stepbrother...husband's load is leaking out of me...while my stepfather watches...and he wants me to help it more! I think I'm in a nightmare! A hot nightmare...but nightmare still!

However her embarrassment, Darcy obeyed her stepfather. She pushed hard, straining every muscle within. A stream of white love seeped out. Contrasting with the pristine pussy, it looked like white paint tossed on a pink canvas, a modern work of art.

Sean looked down in embarrassment. Though his newly hardened cock indicated another force at work. *Not again!* He warned himself.

Shaking in the seat, Darcy kept pushing outward. A bubbling river of stepbrother cum gushed out. The chair edge was soaked in sperm. There was so much, it spilled to the floor.

"Good girl," Tim said. "You can stop now."

Darcy went limp, relaxing her body. She gazed at her stepbrother, staring down at his hard cock. Quite surprised, she suddenly realized he liked it. Dr. Tim Abel stuck a second thinner metal probe through the speculum's border. Aiming all the way back to her cervical wall, he pressed it to Darcy's tight cervical ring.

Grabbing the chair rails, the redhead felt the thin probe enter her cervix. Another clicking sound filled the air, as the tiny speculum opened her tight ring. She moaned and gasped. Stepfather Tim continued without pause. Once the noise stopped, the road to Darcy's womb was fully exposed.

Using the inner light, Dr. Tim Abel took a cotton swab, guiding it deep inside his stepdaughter. As he entered it through the cervical ring, Darcy wiggled at the intense feeling. All the while, clear cervical mucus rushed out, mixed with Sean's sperm.

Tim stuck the cotton swab deeper, swirling and scraping her uterus. The more Darcy squirmed and wiggled, the harder Dr. Abel got. There was something in a patient's submission which turned him on. However, his sexy stepdaughter's submission drove him wild.

Tim removed the swab. He smeared it on a microscope slide. Then, the stepfather mercifully closed and removed the inner speculums from Darcy. "After Sean replaces his sperm sample, both sets of tests will be officially complete. I'll send them to the lab and we'll wait for answers."

"What if...we *can't*?" Sean asked, looking ill.

"Can't...conceive?" Tim responded.

"Right."

"There are many options...in vitro fertilization..."

"No...what I meant to say was...what If *I* can't?" Sean interrupted. "What happens if my sperm isn't good? What if I'm not the man I thought I was?"

"Sean, I told you last time...only 30 percent of the cases are men..."

"Answer me, dad!" Sean insisted.

"For lack of a better answer, Tim said, "Adoption is a fine solution..."

"Fuck!" Sean shouted in frustrated, panicked fear. "I know it's me...my worst fear was always to shoot blanks. My manhood would be crushed...I might as well slap on a dress and call myself Caitlyn!"

Darcy shouted, "Sean Patrick Abel...don't you dare talk like that! You'll always be my man!"

"Son...I don't need to explain to a knowledgeable doctor like yourself...that this happens to many men. It makes them no less of a man!"

Sean rose. "Not *this* man!" he shouted, storming off in fury.

Tim was speechless. He always knew his son was short-fused, though he'd never seen him so defeatist. "We don't even know if he's the cause yet," Dr. Abel said.

"So...what if it's really him?" Darcy asked.

"As I said...adoption..."

"I mean...how will we stop him from losing it?"

Both of them remained silent, staring at each other in worry. Neither of them had an answer, though knew they better find a cure.

*****

Three days passed, the local laboratory sent digital results to Dr. Tim Abel. Upon opening the email, he was pleased to see his stepdaughter's results were excellent for fertility. However, that only left one culprit. With further reading, his worst fears were confirmed. The doctor removed his frameless reading glasses, resting stressed eyes in his hands. "He's screwed!"

Sean Abel *was* the cause of infertility. With a sperm count of 10 million, the odds of egg fertilization were very low. The normal range is 20 million-120 million per millimeter of semen. Although sperm count doesn't make a man, Tim knew his son's alpha pride would destroy him.

However, in vitro was still an option, until Tim read further. Sean's sperm was of poor quality. It was basically, ineffective. The chance of pregnancy would be extremely low. It would break Sean's confidence, his manhood. That was everything to an alpha like him.

Tim was always the one to break the news to patients, though he couldn't destroy the young man. Having lived a life of regret, he didn't want the same for his son. He knew Darcy could handle the news, help break it to Sean. However, there was something more important to tell her first.

It was time to tell Darcy about her mother's death.

*****

"Hey stepdad," the curvy redhead said, hugging Tim Abel. He entered Darcy and Sean's apartment, looking around at the new decor. The walls were painted sage green, little sprigs of fresh flowers were placed throughout.

He also scanned the room for his son. "Sean's...at the office...right?"

"Yeah, booked up today. I can call him, if you want me to. The nurse can flag him down," she said, grabbing her cell phone.

Tim quickly stopped her, "No! I...wanted to come spend time with my daughter. Ever since you moved out, the house has been so quiet."

"I know...it's been strange. It kinda sucks having to make my own breakfast everyday," she smiled. "You spoiled me."

Tim smiled as well, taking another gaze around the room. "Looks good. This place needed a woman's touch. Reminds me of when your..." he paused, finding himself unable to speak the word.

"Mom?" Darcy asked.

"Yes," he said, looking pale, feeling nervous. Although he'd faced risky medical procedures on a daily basis, nothing had shaken his core like the task before him. "Like when *she*...you *both* first moved in. She brought such personality to the place. You have her eye for detail."

"Are you OK, stepdad? You look kinda...green. Can I get you a bottled water?"

"No...no, I'm fine. I promise."

"Oh, then...come here. I've been dying to show someone other than Sean!" she said, leading him by the hand to another room.

Inside the second bedroom, a beautiful display of toys, baby furniture, and a large crib.

Tim turned even more green, feeling sicker. "You haven't even conceived yet."

"I know, but you're gonna help us...right stepdad?"

He exhaled deeply. "Can we talk...in another room? One without...a *crib?*"

Fear filled Darcy's face. "Is the living room OK?"

"Sure."

The two sat down on the couch, Tim tense and crouched. He looked like a man with constipation cramps. "I have some news..."

"We *can't* have children," Darcy said, tears rimming her eyes.

"I wasn't going to say that."

"The look on your face said it for you," Darcy said. Her head sank, a tear rolled down her cheek.

"It's not you."

"Even worse," she said, breaking down in tears.

"At least look into adoption...it's a great thing."

"I'm fine with that, really. But Sean...he's too proud."

Tim put his arm around his stepdaughter, squeezing her tightly. He wiped a tear from her freckled cheek. "I'm so sorry, Darcy. I'd do anything not to see you hurt. Sean either...anything. You're both my children."

"I know, stepdad. I just...always imagined being mother to a newborn. First steps, first words, first smiles...ugh," she shed more tears. "The thing that I *really* wanted...oh forget it...it's so dumb."

"Tell me, please Darcy. Speak your mind."

"If it was a girl...I would've named her Debra...after *mom*," she broke down into her stepfather's chest.

Hearing his deceased wife's name, he was further reminded of his next painful task. *She's distraught, now's not the time to tell her,* he thought. However, he suddenly remembered the therapist's words. *'It's time to tell Darcy the truth. She deserves to know how her mother died, and you deserve to release this secret you've carried around all these years. I know you think avoiding the pain helped you both...but it hasn't.'*

Knowing Shelly Cole was correct, he said, "Darcy...there's something else I have to tell you. It's something you *must* know. Something that may hurt more."

Darcy removed her head from his chest, looking fearful. "Worse than a childless future and broken husband? What could that be?"

"It's about *your* mother. It's something I never told you..."

The redhead's heartbreak was suddenly replaced by shock. "OMG...you poisoned her!"

"What? No! My God...why would you say that?"

"Sorry, I've read too many eBooks. Please...just tell me."

Tim took a deep breath, exhaling even deeper. "The accident...the night she was hit head on...it was by a *drunk* driver."

Darcy turned pale, she trembled. "That's so horrible."

"You can hate me. I won't blame you...I already hate myself for it," he said, rising to leave.

"Stepdad...wait!" she begged, grabbing onto his arm, pulling him back into his seat. She hugged him tightly, "Thank you."

Now Tim was the one in pale shock. "You're thanking me? Why? I hid information from you. It was your right to know."

"Honestly, stepdad...I don't think I could've handled it back then. I was just a kid...my world shattered. Growing up without a mother was hard enough, though knowing she was killed that way...would've broken me. Please, don't hate yourself...you did it to protect me!" she said, hugging the man tighter.

He hugged her back, equally as tight. Like the therapist said, a piece of his heart was healed. Unfortunately, a large majority of it still ached deeply. The ghost, which haunted him, was still present. "I'll always protect you, my red rose." He kissed her on the head.

"Did the guy die too?"

"No...he was barely hurt. He got a slap on the wrist...a liberal fucking judge saying a lack of love from his parents caused him to drink. He was given probation...court ordered to write a letter."

"Are you joking?"

"I couldn't joke about the punk who ruined our lives."

"What did the letter say?"

Dr. Abel pulled a folded letter from his pocket. It was crumbled, taped together. Although a decade had passed, the wear wasn't from time. The damage was from Tim's angry assault upon it. "Read it for yourself. I've read it too many times. It sickens me every time."

Darcy took the shaking letter from her stepfather's hands. Her hands were shaking as much.

The letter read: *Dear Mr. Abel,*

Sorry man, for driving drunk and killing your wife. I usually can handle my liquor, though I guess I was wrong in this case. My car was damaged too, so I lost something too. Anyway, as the court told me to do, I wrote this to say I'm sorry for doing what I did.

Mike Robertson

"Wow! That guy's an asswipe! He could care less about what he did! Why did you keep this? It would make any person bitter!"

Tim's dark face cringed. He thought about her question. "In a sick way...it was my comfort."

"So...you liked it?"

"Oh, no Darcy...not comfort in the way you may think. With every flippant word, my need for revenge was served more."

A look of realization suddenly crossed her face. "That's why you can't move on...it's why you still hurt so much."

"Perhaps," he said, taking the letter back.

Darcy hung on to the letter, refusing to give it back. "Let it go, stepdad. Don't keep torturing yourself. It's not fair to you...to keep living it everyday. At some point, you have to just move on!"

"I need it!" he shouted, pulling at it harder. The letter tore again, Darcy's half floated to the floor. "No!" Tim dove for it, piecing it back together in desperation.

Seeing her stepfather in frantic panic, Darcy ran to get tape. Kneeling to him on the floor, she handed it over. He grabbed it, quickly taping the letter back together, adding yet another layer to the artifact. Once it was reassembled, he placed it to his thumping heart, reclining flat on the floor.

Tears fell from Darcy's eyes, as she lay with him, placing her head upon his chest. "I'm sorry, I didn't mean to rip it."

"It's OK, baby. You're not the one whose sins need resolving. The scumbag took her life...we can never get it back."

"No, we can't, stepdad," Darcy said, placing a hand on her stomach. "I hoped to create another...a life to honor her memory. I guess, that dream's over too."

A flash of determination struck Tim. "Not if I can help it."

"But I thought you said...Sean's sperm couldn't be cured."

"I did."

"Then how can you get me pregnant?"

"Anyway I have to. Do you still trust me...to do the right thing for you?"

"Always."

"Then don't give up. That dream...will come true."

*****

Tim Abel's car pulled up to a decent home in a pleasant neighborhood. No stranger to the sight, it wasn't the first time he'd been there. A few years back, he did an internet search for the drunk driver's name. Knowing his target was 34-years old now, only one matched his criteria. After a visual confirmation, he studied his subject like a scholar to ancient text.

An SUV pulled into the home's driveway. Out walked a man in his mid-thirties. He wore a white shirt and tie. His hair was slicked back, definitely a productive member of society. To the average eye, it was a far cry from a drunken college kid. Nothing physical remained of the slacker's drinking days. Though to Tim Abel, the kid's face was unforgettable. He had a look in his eyes of entitled arrogance. The smirk on his face was ever-present.

Dr. Abel remembered sitting in the courtroom, seeing the drunk's smirk on full display. Even awaiting sentencing, the college kid rolled his eyes in boredom. Throughout, the kid was disinterested. Tim felt like he was in that court again, watching the same spoiled kid walk virtually free.

Upon hearing the sentence, the kid laughed, hugging his high-priced family lawyer. While one family celebrated, another stewed in anger. However, the only family member present was Tim himself. Not even Sean was allowed to go, remaining clueless to the present day.

Tim gazed around at the houses, cringing in sickness. *Pleasantville...a pretty house, trimmed lawn, white picket fence. The guilty fucker gets to live the American dream...while my innocent wife rots in a grave. His kids get to hug their father every day. His wife gets to kiss her husband each night. Why is life so fucking unfair? Why do good people die while scum get to live? He took her from us. Damn it...I'm going to take him from them. Eye for an eye...tooth for a tooth.*

*****

"Hello again, Dr. Abel," Dr. Shelly Cole said, her blond hair sparkling in the bronze room light.

Tim paused momentarily, struck again by the resemblance to his deceased wife. "Hi, Debra...I'm mean, Dr. Cole," he said, shaking her hand. His mind was clearly distracted, face tensed.

"Take a seat."

Tim sat down on the couch. He was uptight, unfocused.

Shelly continued. "So, did we make progress with Darcy?"

"We did," he said in a depressed voice

"You'll have to excuse me Dr. Abel...but the tone of your voice doesn't exactly convey progress."

"It's not *that*...in fact, it couldn't have gone any better. She actually thanked me. I have to admit, Dr. Cole...but...you were right. I should've told her sooner."

The therapist smiled, "I think we're beyond the point of formalities, doctor. Call me, Shelly. May I call you, Tim?"

A surprised, but pleased look crossed Dr. Abel's face. "Please do." He silently wondered, *Does she do this with all her patients...or am I just...special? Oh...special can denote retardation in this field...oh don't be ridiculous. You're a highly educated man!*

"Great. I figure...if I expect a patient to trust me with their innermost thoughts...I can call them by their first name," she said.

The look of hope melted off Tim's face. *Not so special after all. Who was I kidding anyway...therapist's don't date their patients.* "Noted. Shelly it is."

"So, Tim...tell me, what else is troubling you today?"

"It's Darcy...a different issue than the drunk. Actually, it's more my son...than stepdaughter."

"Marital issues?"

"Not of their own making. Fertility trouble."

"I see. Well, I'm not the one to council *you* in that area," Shelly said. Tim smiled at her. Now Shelly was the one to pause, gazing deeply into his eyes.

"Is something wrong, Shelly?"

"No...not at all. Please, go on with your story."

"The thing is...my son doesn't know he's the reason for failure."

"I'm assuming...as his doctor, you'll tell him."

Tim stayed quiet for a moment, looking downward. "I will."

"Is it a fixable issue?"

Again, Dr. Abel paused in hesitation. "I believe it is," he said untruthfully.

"Then fix it."

"I plan on it."

"The look in your eyes tells me...it won't be conventional."

"You're good."

Shelly's mind went to many scenarios, though one seemed impossible yet probable. "I hope I'm not as good as you think...because something tells me...I don't want to know."

"OK, it turns out...you're *really* good. And trust me, you don't."

She hadn't dared speak it in detail. "Do you really think that's wise, doctor?"

"He can't have kids...would never be able to live with failure."

"What's worse...his body failing him...or his father...twice in one life?"

"You wouldn't understand...it's an alpha thing. Pride will kill him well before anything I do."

"Ah...one of those macho men. Very tough nuts to crack. Is he the only reason?"

Tim remained silent for a moment. "Yes."

"Tim...be honest."

"I don't know. Maybe...it's something inside me. Something urging...even begging me to act boldly. I can't explain it."

"Just promise me something, Tim. Whatever it is you're going to do...please, really think it over. It's something you can't undo. Will you ever tell him?"

"I don't know."

"I'd assume Darcy would have to know."

He remained quiet again, "I told you...I'm still undecided on the matter. Haven't thought out the details."

"OK, fair enough. Speaking of Darcy...let's talk about your opening up to her. From the looks of it...it didn't heal your pain."

"I must really look like shit to you."

"No, Tim. I'm reading your emotion...and it tells me you're in pain."

He exhaled in defeat, "Yes, the pain and anger's still there."

"It's OK. We'll keep digging...until that pain goes away."

"But I know the answer...I've known for years. The only question is...should I do it?"

"Do what, Tim?"

He took a deep breath, exhaling afterward. "The dark thoughts."

"Enacting them," she said, fighting her own face from twitching.

"Right...enacting them. He needs to die...for me to live."

Dr. Shelly Cole's face turned pale. Though, the look was less outrage than it was conflict. "Tim...there's nothing wrong with having these thoughts...these fantasies."

"It's not fantasy...once I make it reality. I need to kill him...to avenge my wife! I need to make him hurt...like she hurt! Break every fucking bone in his body...the way her bones were. I need to burn him...the way *she* burned!"

"Years have passed...he may have moved...maybe karma caught up to him...maybe he's dead?"

"Mike Robertson's alive and doing well. Everyday for the last decade...I've gazed at the court ordered letter. His signature...looped letters...big bold print...like some celebrity signing an autograph. Fucking narcissist."

"From the sounds of it...you know more about him than his name, signature. Tell me, Tim...have you been...watching him?"

Dr. Abel's face was flushed, eyes trained to the floor. His voice got darker than it ever had. "I know where he lives...what kind of car he drives...his kids' school...wife's name...the color lipstick she wears on her happy smile..."

"So you're stalking them."

"I'm watching *his* life...the one I never got to have."

"So your mind's made up...you plan on killing him," she stated in a stressed voice.

Tim paused, body tensed like a man in the electric chair. "I can't say."

"Don't know...or can't say?"

"Both. You'll call the authorities."

"Doctor patient confidentiality...I can't...would lose my license."

"In cases of premeditation...we both know *that* privilege is moot."

"Then I *won't!*" she boldly and convincingly declared.

"Why not?"

Shelly's heart raced, pulse pounded, clear streams of sweat wet her skin. She ignored his question. "Will taking his life heal your pain?"

"I'm beyond the point of lectures, Shelly. As a therapist...I know it's your job to talk me out of it..."

"I'm *not* talking you out of it. I'm asking you...will it heal your pain?"

Shock crossed Tim's face. "Aren't you the shrink here?"

"Even the best therapists...lack answers vital to their own lives. We're still human beings."

"How's my situation vital to your life?"

"I lost my husband," she admitted.

"I'm so sorry to hear that...truly. But...what does *that* have to do with my need for vengeance? Could you enlighten me on that?"

A streak of shame struck Shelly. *Oh my God...I've committed the unthinkable therapist sin. I've become the patient!* "I'm sorry, Tim...I need to cut this session short," she said, standing.

Another look of surprise filled Tim's face. Though intrigue was the greater emotion. He stood up, saying, "I'm sorry, Shelly. I didn't mean to..."

"No...it's me, not you. Though, I have to say...I don't think the first name thing was a good idea. We should return to our respective titles."

"OK, Dr. Cole. Can I just ask..."

"Dr. Abel...I'm the one who's supposed to ask the questions. Now please, sir...I must end this session for today."

"When should I return?"

"When I ask you to," she said, shuffling through old paperwork, avoiding eye contact.

Finally getting the message, Tim headed for the door. Before exiting, he stopped. "Whatever I said to offend you...I'm sorry."

"I'm the one who's sorry, doctor," she said, failing to offer further detail.

With those last words, Tim Abel exited her office. He never expected to see her again, though it didn't matter. His mind was already made up. *I know what I must do to end this pain.*

I need to end one life...and create another.

CHAPTER FOUR

"Put on the gown and sit in the chair. Dr. Abel will be right in to see you," the nurse told Darcy in the exam room.

The redhead's eyebrows rose in surprise. "No, he just...wanted to talk...I think."

"I just follow the doctor's instructions, Mrs. Abel. He said to put on the gown and get in the chair. That's all I know," the nurse said, exiting the room.

Why would he do that? He already examined me...my results came back fine. Did he find a way to cure Sean's problem? He promised that I'd carry the Abel seed...no matter what he had to do. Oh shit! He's an Abel too. Na...he'd never do that. I mean, Sean would lose his mind. Though...I doubt he'd be as heart broken as a childless future. Maybe...he'd never even know. Stepdad looks like an older version of Sean, the resemblance would be similar. I can't say I'd mind having sex with him...as the anal was damn good. AM I

NUTS? He'd never ask such a thing anyway! Grow up, Darcy...this is crazy talk!

Forcing thoughts from her head, she removed her clothes. Slipping the paper gown over feminine curves, she sat in the gyno chair. Waiting nervously, she bit her bottom lip in fear. As a knock sounded on the door, her anxiousness only grew more.

Entering the room, he paused at the mere sight of his stepdaughter. It wasn't her appearance that spooked him. He feared what he had to do. "Hello Darcy," he finally said, walking over to hug her. It had been a few weeks since her last test, timed to the day by the ovulation calendar.

The look in Tim's eyes spoke louder than his voice. It was as if he'd told her his plan without speaking. Their thoughts synced, even though they hadn't quite processed it yet. "Hi stepdad," Darcy said.

"You're probably wondering why I called you here...asked you to wear a gown."

"It's OK, stepdad," she said. "It doesn't matter why. Just...save us. Save Sean from himself."

Empowerment seized Dr. Abel's face. Darcy's words cemented his plan, all but granting verbal permission to enact it. *I can't let her carry the blame...burden of hiding a lifelong secret. I'll carry it for her.* Without speaking, he headed over to a cabinet. He removed something, slipping it in his pocket. Darcy didn't see what it was. "I told Sean...just minutes ago," he said.

"You did?" she asked in shock. "Did he freak out? He must be hurting right now, angry, embarrassed to know the truth..."

"I didn't tell him the truth."

"No?"

"I told him his results were fine...like his wife. I lied."

"So he'll just keep trying...and failing? Is that really the answer, stepdad?"

Tim slowly approached Darcy. "Put your feet in the stirrups," he said in a dominant tone.

Darcy's heart pounded. She wondered what was going to happen. Although scared, she hoped for him to seed her. *I know this is so wrong...soooo wrong! But...it will save Sean...plus make my dream come true. My husband can't be fixed. I can lie to myself and say I don't want to feel my stepfather inside my pussy...but it would be pointless. I do want it. He felt amazing in my ass...his cum did too. Will I ever be able to forgive myself for allowing it?* Darcy obediently put her feet in the stirrups, parting her thighs like Moses' did the Red Sea. With her feminine feet firmly in the stirrups, Darcy awaited action.

One last exhale exited Tim's lungs. Shifting all thoughts of consequence aside, he felt her forehead. Removing a glass thermometer, he lubed the tip, along with her asshole. As it was slipped into her sphincter, Darcy squirmed in the chair.

After waiting a minute, he removed the glass probe from the dark garden. Studying it, his timing was right on. *A slight rise in temperature...she's ovulating again. It's now or never.*

Next, he opened an alcohol swab. Cleansing her ass cheek with one hand, he carefully removed a syringe from his pocket. Hiding it behind his medical coat, he neared his stepdaughter.

Finally ready to end the anxious wonderment, Darcy asked, "Can I ask...what you plan on doing to me, stepdad?"

Without speaking another word, Tim Abel jabbed the needle's spear into Darcy's ass cheek. Spread in the gyno chair, Darcy moaned loudly. "What are you doing...step...dad!" she slurred, feeling the heavy rush of medicine squirt into her. Her eyelids fought to stay open, fluttering. "Stepdad...I feel kinda dizzy," she said in a whispered voice.

"Shhh." Darcy's stepfather placed a latex finger to her full lips. "Just let the medicine take you away. Surrender your total submission to me...and I'll save you both."

"Please...tell me why," her breathy voice gushed. Darcy's eyeballs rolled upwards, last signs of lucidness faded. "I'm so sleepy."

"Shhh," he said again, covering her mouth, pinching her nostrils. The lack of oxygen helped her float faster into twilight. He knew she'd first enter a stage of true sleep. Within minutes, she'd exit from slumber, feeling every sexual stroke with heightened pleasure. She'd remain confused, eventually awakening to a cloudy reality.

Tim thought, *She deserves to experience her journey into motherhood, even if it feels like a dream. She never asked me to do this...therefore...she'll never have to live with the guilt accompanying the aftermath.*

Darcy's lids closed. Her body went fully limp as she officially entered the sleep stage. Feet remained propped in the stirrups, legs spread. Her stepfather leaned inward, kissing her forehead.

Dr. Abel lowered his pants, freeing an 8-inch cock of steel. Tossing all guilt aside, a hunger to seed his stepdaughter outweighed all emotion. He walked towards her smooth thighs, sliding his cock-head along her sleepy slit.

His thick member engorged more, girth expanded in arousal. Every vein popped in strain, begging to feel Darcy's creamy pussy. He placed the bulbous head against her honey hole, pushing inward. In moments, his manly helmet popped into the poon paradise.

A satisfied moan sounded from Dr. Abel. With Darcy asleep, her vaginal tension completely relaxed. However, the deeper he sank into her, the closer her 19-year-old natural tightness hugged his rod.

Soon, all 8-inches were inside her. Tim's face tensed from the unbelievable pleasure. Not only was the sensation soft and sensual, but also a dream come true. After anally pleasing her on his marital bed, he'd planned to claim her pussy. However, he'd erupted, missing his chance. Ever since that night, he'd imagined the feeling. His wish was granted.

He began fucking her, slow steady strokes. His cock was awash in her sweetness. With each passionate entrance, he stared at her resting face. It was so beautiful, so peaceful. Her lips were so wet and full.

The mere sight of her limp curvy body made him harder. Of course, the fact that she was helpless to his sexual whims drove him wild. Chemical chains kept her prisoner to his sexual orders.

His forward slides turned to crashes. Darcy's body jolted from the landings. Tim held her ankles in the stirrups, keeping her safely in-place. His balls spanked stepdaughter ass cheeks, ramming his hardness as deeply as possible.

Still staring at her lips, he had to kiss them. Leaning inward, he kept his fucking motion moving. Stepfather's lips engulfed stepdaughter's. The set on her mouth were as sweet as her pussy flaps. After just one peck, Darcy's body began to gently rouse.

Her sleepy lips fought to return the loving gesture. It couldn't, though Dr. Abel performed enough for them both. Lip locks transformed into French kissing. Passion filled Darcy's partially conscious body. It began to regain some control, her tongue joined in on the action. Together, stepfather and stepdaughter did the forbidden dance.

Feeling his cock swell, Dr. Abel broke the kiss. He stood straight again, pounding away at his stepdaughter's pink pussy. Even though cumming was the purpose of his mission, he fought from doing so. *This is the only time I'll ever get to do this. I don't want it to end...I must hold on! It feels too damn good!*

Needing a distraction, he turned to Darcy's feminine feet. Licking the sole of her right foot, he rose up the sensitive center. His fucking rhythm remained steadily hard, tongue licked and sucked on her foot. He engulfed her toes with his mouth, biting each one. Tim crashed harder into her.

The first sounds of pleasure trickled from Darcy's captive mouth. A ghostly tickle fluttered through her body, teasing her partially conscious mind. Thick cock invaded her dreams, as a pleasurable ache dragged her from drugged sleep itself.

Darcy's eyelids gently opened. *Is this even real?* She wondered. *Am I dreaming? I'm so confused...I just know I want more. It feels so good, I want my stepfather to own me...knock me up.* The sleeping beauty shut her eyes again, lost in a sexual fog.

Dr. Abel's manly member pounded deeper into the redhead's pussy. Darcy was so wet and creamy, her love juice dripped down his swinging balls. Reaching out for her breasts, Tim grabbed handfuls of the C-cups. Tugging and pulling on erect nipples, electric pulses of pained-pleasure shot through her body. He smashed his stepdaughter's velvet tunnel with more vigor. Switching to the left foot, his saliva spilled down it.

His hands worked her breasts like manic marionettes. The crazed sensations further awakened Darcy's senses. Feeling the cock ram her deepest vaginal depths, her pussy was inflamed with sexual fire.

Darcy's arousal built like a slow-moving tsunami. Many small waves of pleasure united in an unworldly splash. With one last cock blow, the redheaded stepdaughter erupted in erotic explosion. In her head, she screamed louder than she ever had before, orgasming to a level never experienced.

She felt herself rumble, shake, and grab onto the chair rails. Warm chills crossed her sweaty skin, feeling her stepfather's cock continuously pound her pussy. Darcy felt her voice speak, "Stepdad...cum inside me! Give me your baby!"

Of course, she didn't actually make a sound or movement. Captive to chemical sleep, the ballet of lust remained trapped inside her pleasurable poon prison. Though her verbal muzzle didn't matter. Her unspoken request was about to be fulfilled.

"Fuck!" Dr. Abel shouted, freeing Darcy's cute feet from his mouth. Her wet, teenage pussy choked and milked his cock, nearly begging for cum itself. He drove into her, forced to fire his heavy white load.

His deep manly grunt filled the air. His white medical coat floated behind him in the air-conditioned breeze, muscular ass cheeks stiffened. The 54-year-old stepfather filled his 19-year-old stepdaughter with a forbidden flood.

Darcy reached the fine line between sleep and control, her body shook violently. Feeling her stepfather's seed made her orgasm again, harder than the first. Each load felt bigger than the last, squirted hard and deep into her womb. The more it filled her, the more cum she craved.

Tim Abel's balls were nearly drained of life, firing every single sperm they could produce. A ring of white formed around the base of his cock and Darcy's pussy lips. There was so much, it overflowed.

After his last squirt coated the curvy patient, he quickly withdrew. Darcy's eyes jolted open, free from twilight. However, a surprised stab of the syringe's needle returned her to darkness.

The captive dream-state continued on. Tim would claim her womb again and again, shooting Abel sperm deep into the sexy redhead. The stepfather had successfully seeded his stepdaughter's womb. More importantly, Darcy would never have to face the guilt of consenting to it.

Finally able to ejaculate no more, the step-doctor adjusted the stirrups. Bringing the steel spreaders tightly together, he shut Darcy's legs, trapping his cum inside her fertile womb. Then, he lowered her gyno chair downward, tilting it at a diagonal angle. Her head was aimed at the floor, pussy in the air. The frothing cum was forced downward into the womb. It forced the army of white life through the cervical ring, into the uterus, and right for the ovary's bulls eye.

By the time Darcy awoke with a gasp, she was being watched by the nurse. Returned to an upright, seated position and dressed in her clothes, confusion overcame her. "Stepdad?"

"He's with another patient. I'll walk you out," the nurse said.

The redhead nodded, following the nurse to the exit. *What happened in here? My mind is so hazy. Did he really have sex with me...or was it just a dream? I couldn't ask him...would be too embarrassing. Was it as hot as it felt? Did he really knock me up? Is it wrong that I remember liking it?*

Is it wrong...that I hope it was real?

*****

Dr. Shelly Cole kissed her husband's cheek. She was sitting next to him in the passenger seat. Darkness and fog masked the chilly night. Headlight beams were swallowed by thick atmosphere.

"I love you so much, handsome," she said, gazing at her husband lovingly.

"Not as much as I love you, beautiful," he responded, keeping his eyes responsibly on the road ahead.

"We'll call it a tie," she declared with a smile.

"I'd call that fair. Though, I swear to you...that love will never die." His voice seeped with passion.

Shelly's husband's words skipped her ears, heading straight for the heart. A warmth surrounded her, mesmerized by his deep love. "Mine either. Though...can you make room for one more?"

He gasped. "You're...pregnant?"

"I am," she said with a beaming smile.

A quick turn of his head met her lips. "I'll love you both with all my heart...on this earth and after."

Suddenly, a pair of headlights shot through the fog, getting brighter with each moment. "A car's...coming...at us..."

CRASH! It happened in a flash of a moment, though to Shelly's eyes, it appeared to never end. Time slowed to a death crawl. A pickup truck roared through fog like a ghost train. Shelly and husband were traveling at the speed limit of 65 MPH. The truck barreled forward at 100 MPH.

The collision was punishing, impact horrifying. They hit so hard, steel bent like hammered butter. While the truck's engine remained intact, Shelly's Toyota engine was crushed.

Though as bad as the outside damage was, the inside impact was deadly. Too frightened to scream, the couple froze in suspended disbelief. Glass shattered inward, peppering them with dagger-like shards.

Each of their bodies were hurled forward, yanked upon like rag dolls. Although seat belts protected the couple from being ejected, the force broke bones instantly. Shelly saw the massive truck heading to crush her.

Right before the vehicle could end her life, the car took a rip-roaring spin. Her husband turned the car away from her, towards himself. The truck's weight was shifted towards his side, crushing the dashboard into his chest. Speeding forward, the offensive vehicle shoved Shelly's car off road, into an old oak tree.

A piece of metal debris hit Shelly Cole in the forehead. Everything went black, though her ears remained in operation. The sound of more grinding steel was heard. Her car was pulled forward in motion. It spun out again, as if flung by the hand of a giant. The dark, terrifying ride was like a deadly *Space Mountain.* Another loud bang shook her, finally stopping. Then, the sound of a rusty dying engine drove off.

Shelly's eyes opened as if awakening from a nightmare. She gazed out the glassless window, on the opposite roadside of her blackout. The sound of distant sirens filled the air.

Reality started to drift back. The nightmare was real. Quickly turning her head, she was face to face with her dead husband. Shaking in traumatic fear, she tried to scream, though only air came out. One of her husband's eyes was out of socket, a trail of blood spilled from his open mouth. A glass dagger pierced his throat. Though the worst thing of all: a metal rod impaled his loving heart.

"AHHHH!" Shelly screamed in traumatic horror. She was not covered in blood, but sweat. The professional therapist wasn't facing her husband, but a ghostly memory. Dr. Cole wasn't in a destroyed car, she was in her bedroom. Although she wasn't currently living a nightmare, she'd already lived it.

The night terrors were nothing new, they reoccurred every night. Each one felt more real, each detail more chilling. For a moment, she reached out to touch her deceased husband's face, swearing he was physically there. Though he'd just disappear like liquid smoke.

She rolled off the bed, landing in a fetal position. "Go away...make me forget...take the pain with you!" she cried. The more she begged, the stronger her memories played on.

First it was her being welded out of the steel coffin of car. Then came the cutting of her seat belt. She remembered grabbing onto the strap, begging the EMT workers, "Please...let me stay with him. He needs me! My husband needs me! The baby needs its father!" The medics had to pry her hands off the strap, wrestle her from the car, and strap her to the gurney.

She recalled seeing her husband's blood-covered body. The horrific sight continued, as he was cut and freed from the driver's seat. As his torso was removed, his legs were severed. The bent steering column had cut his body in two.

Then her memories skipped to the hospital. The doctors entered, unable to stare her in the face. "I've lost the baby," she said coldly, emotionlessly.

"I'm sorry, Mrs. Cole...we believe it was the force from the seatbelt...though it's too hard to say for sure. We're sorry for your losses," he said. "We'll provide grief therapy..."

"I *am* a therapist," she said in a deep monotone voice. Clearly, shock set in, turning all emotion off. "There's nothing they can tell me...that I don't already know. Leave me alone."

"I'll give you some time," he said, turning to exit with his team.

"Doctor," she said.

The man stopped, turning to address her. "Yes, Mrs. Cole?"

"I need to know...what happened to the man who hit us?"

The doctor paused. "He's dead. We found his demolished vehicle down the road. He drove into another tree," he said, turning to leave again.

"He was drunk," she said as a matter of fact.

"Get some rest. We'll talk about that later..."

"Tell me. It's my right to know."

The doctor stopped, keeping his back to her. "He was."

Shelly's flashback ended there. Curled in a ball on her bedroom floor, tears fell from her eyes like acid rain. Learning the driver was drunk was as painful as the loss itself. "My family died for nothing!" she screamed. "I wanted revenge! I was owed it, damn it! Owed something!" She broke down in manic hurt.

The usual suicidal thoughts plagued her, though one thing had kept her going through the years: vengeance. It seemed impossible for her to get, since the drunk died before *she* could. However, it suddenly became obtainable again. It wasn't her direct target, though a scumbag nonetheless. The therapist in her knew it was wrong, though the wife needed it.

Shelly Cole came to a decision. She wiped her tears again, stood tall, and clinched her fists. "The bastard must die for his sins. For Tim's pain...and my own."

*****

Dr. Tim Abel lay in bed. Weeks expired since seeding his stepdaughter, they hadn't spoken since. During the span of time, many thoughts crossed his mind. *Will my seed take hold? Does she even know I did it? Does she hate me for doing it? Will she ever tell my son?*

However, his usual obsession also grew greater. He gazed at pictures of the drunk driver's house. Although he photographed it a few years ago, the image brought him comfort when unable to stalk in person. Having walked the building's perimeter, he timed when the home was occupied and vacant. Work was 9-5 on weekdays, usually running 10 minutes late. Wife and kids left at 8 AM, were home at 6 PM, often on schedule.

It gives me an hour...morning or night. An hour to kill, he thought in his mind. *Then...I can deal with his wife and kids.* A chill crossed his skin, fright seized his body. It wasn't the thought of taking lives which scared him; it was his lack of remorse which did. His dark thoughts started feeling normal. Killing his enemy felt more holy than letting him live. There was no turning back. Teetering on the very edge of action, all he needed was a slight push.

A sudden knock at the door startled him. He looked at the clock, wondering, *Who the hell would be knocking at 3 AM? Darcy or Sean would likely call.* Rising from the bed, he crept to the front entrance. Turning on the light, he peeked through the peephole. *OK...this is likely a dream. Wet dream, perhaps?* He wondered in hope.

He opened the door, expecting to awaken. Instead, he was greeted by his guest. "Hello, Tim," Shelly Cole said. "May I come in?"

The speechless Dr. Abel nodded, having no words. The sexy blond therapist entered, as he followed her inside. "How'd you..."

"Your medical history forms...the line that said address."

"I should've figured. The question I should really ask...why are you here? Why at this time?"

"I'm sorry...this was incredibly rude, impulsive, and unprofessional. I could lose my license for this. I'll go," she said, heading towards the door.

The strong older man grabbed her arm. He pulled her into him forcefully, the two crashed together. Their eyes met, lips neared. A magnetic force nearly drew them. "You're not going anywhere," he declared.

Used to holding and needing the power, Dr. Shelly Cole suddenly felt like the submissive patient. "OK, doctor...I'll stay."

He kept hold of her, unwilling to let go. "So tell me...why here, why now?"

"Because I had to answer the question...my own question," she said.

"What question? What couldn't wait until a decent hour?" Tim asked in confusion.

"Will killing *him* heal *your* pain?" she recited.

Tim's face grew tense. "Will it?"

She looked him dead in the eyes, heated with anger. She boldly said, "It'll heal *our* pain."

"Our?"

Shelly exhaled, "I told you I lost my husband. I never told you...it was the same way you lost your wife. I lost my unborn child with him. I saw unspeakable horror unfold before my eyes."

A look of deep pain filled Tim Abel. "I'm so sorry."

"The fault doesn't belong to you. You're a victim...as I am," she stated. "I spent years in my therapy practice trying to answer this very question...I couldn't find it. Though when you walked in...everything changed. This *has* to be the way. We can't bring them back. We can't resurrect life...though damn it...we can take it."

Tim finally had clarity in his mind. The last blockade to vengeance was gone. Shelly looked at Tim, waiting for a response. He stared into her eyes, grabbing the back of her blond head. Pulling her into him, he kissed her lips passionately. The feeling was amazing to them both. It was like a fire of love, once snuffed, was suddenly rekindled. Hit like a bolt of lightning, both of them pulled away. Unsure and afraid of the pulsing pound inside their hearts, they returned their focus to the matter at hand.

Forcing the feelings away, Shelly asked, "How will you do it? Fists? A knife? A gun?"

A new shade of darkness crossed Dr. Abel's face. "Anything I can get my hands on."

Shelly shut her eyes, hoping beyond words that it would cure her pain. If it didn't, not only would she be an accessory to murder, she'd have led her patient to commit it. At that moment, neither of them cared about consequence. They wanted revenge, and at 5 PM, they'd have it. "Do you have room for one more weapon?" she asked.

"Like what?"

"Me."

CHAPTER FIVE

Dr. Abel's car pulled up to the drunk driver's home. The low winter sun neared its early set time. Tim gazed at his watch, seeing the hands form 5 o'clock. With a usual ten-minute window, he awaited his prey's arrival.

Both Shelly and Tim sat silently. The blond therapist stared at Tim's bag, seeing an iron-poker, blowtorch, scalpel, rope, and a can of gasoline. For all her vengeful fantasizing over the years, reality felt much different.

The therapist's inner-voice begged her, *You must stop this. The blood will be on your hands. You took an oath, have a responsibility to uphold. Instead, you betrayed it. Shut up!* Shelly's dark side took-over. *You owe this to* your husband...*to yourself. Killing this piece of shit will make things right, allow you to sleep at night. Make him suffer like you suffered!* Forcing all thoughts from her mind, Shelly asked, "Shouldn't we go inside before he gets home? Take him by surprise?"

"They've got a house alarm. He only arms it when no one's home...and when he sleeps at night. Don't worry, he takes a shower immediately after work."

"You certainly know him well."

"A predator must find its prey's weakness and strength before attacking. It's crucial to success."

Shelly nodded, "I guess I've never...actually hunted human before."

Another minute of tense silence passed. Tim asked, "How were you able to move on...after seeing such things? I mean, I had a stepdaughter to cling to, a son...but you lost everything."

Shelly was quiet, exhaling before speaking. "I may appear physically here to you, doctor...but understand this...I never left *that* vehicle. I died there alongside my family. Yes, I was alone...I'm still alone. I hide within. I wanted a child so badly, though couldn't betray my husband like that."

"Did you try to date?"

"How could I love again...when I can lose it all as easily? Emotional investment takes everything...and I have nothing to deposit."

"So you're no different than I am."

"Sadly, I'm not."

"Should you really be charging me then?"

A sly smirk crossed Shelly's face. "Consider it on the house, doctor."

The sun sank, darkness barely kissed sky. A pair of headlights shined, as a car pulled into the enemy's home.

"It's time," Tim said, locking his eyes on the prey.

*****

Mike Robertson let the water cascade his freshly shaven face. Shiny clean, he stepped up to the mirror's reflection, flashing his pearly white veneers. After lotioning his skin, he gelled his hair back. The high-maintenance man valued his appearance above all else in life. The only glare in his dark eyes was vanity, remorse unknown to them.

Blowing a kiss to his reflection, he repeated, "Number one," holding a finger up. If anything was clear about him, he was as much a douchebag as his younger days. Exiting the room, he headed into the kitchen. Opening up the refrigerator, he grabbed a Corona beer. As he closed the swinging door, a stranger appeared behind it.

Crack! A fist flew at his face. Pained moans sounded from the 34-year-old as he crashed to the ground. The bottle smashed beside him. Beer suds sprayed his body, stung his eyes. A few glass shards pierced his skin. Wiping his eyes clear, Mike the drunk, saw Tim standing over him. Shelly stood behind Tim.

Dr. Abel held the iron fireplace poker; Shelly Cole dangled a line of rope from her hand. The panicked Mike Robertson grabbed the broken beer bottle. He swung it at Tim's leg. Alert and focused, Tim swung the metal poker, blocking and smashing the glass bottle toward the enemy.

Then he whacked Mike's hand with the iron rod, breaking the remaining bottleneck in the punk's palm. The drunk driver screamed in pain, glass cracking inside hand, bones breaking as well. Tim Abel raised the poker, finally ready to smite the demon.

Desperate and afraid, the drunk driver kicked Tim's knees. Dr. Abel fell backwards, dropping the poker. The younger guy leapt on the older doctor, swinging at his face. "You fucker!" he shouted, continuing to bludgeon his mystery assailant.

WHACK! The iron poker hit drunken Mike's head. The arrogant enemy was knocked back, flung off Tim. Before the doctor could recover, Shelly continued the assault. First she hit his nose with the iron weapon, breaking it. Swinging wildly, she hit the man in the ribs. "Die! Die! Die! Let our pain die with you!" she shouted, crying her eyes out. Even then, her assault continued, years of frustration and anger flowing. She kept swinging until collapsing.

Dr. Abel caught her fall, hugging her tightly. "It'll all be over soon...but not yet," he said with cold assurance in his voice.

Hearing Tim's words, the bloodied drunk driver desperately crawled away. "Fuck off!" he yelled, slipping on his own blood.

"I'm going to need the rope," he told Shelly, gently setting her down. Taking the line, Tim pursued his fleeing prisoner.

Shelly broke down in deeper tears, realizing that her pain hadn't dissolved at all. *It's not gone like I hoped. Will killing him finally do it? I know better than this...I've seen past victims...it didn't work for them. Why me? How will I live with it? How will Tim live with it? It's too late now...he's on a mission...and no one can stop him.*

Tim slowly trailed his prey, walking the crimson path. The drunk driver's trembling hand reached for the doorknob. Right before he could touch it, the rope was wrapped around Mike's neck.

Yanked away from escape, Tim secured the enemy's slicked, stiffened hair. Dragged back to a kitchen chair, the drunk was forcefully bound to the structure. The arrogant man spit blood out at Tim. Instead of wiping it, Dr. Abel merely smeared it on his cheeks, like war paint.

Shelly watched in wonderment. *Is he losing his mind...or just trying to make the man think he's lost it?*

Another closed fist hit Mike's eye, immediately swelling it shut. The enemy let out a pained shout. "Why the fuck are you doing this? You want money? Man, I got plenty of it. I'll give you all of it...just fucking let me go."

A crazed laugh sounded from Tim Abel. Once a usually reserved man, years of bottled up anger were unleashed. Although he melted down after facing his feelings for Darcy, it was now way beyond that. He was losing all control of himself. The taunting laughter continued for minutes straight, getting louder and crazier. "You think this is about money?" Tim shouted.

"I don't give a fuck what it is, asswipe! I'll have the cops bust your ass either way!" Mike said arrogantly. Even in an imprisoned, pained state, he still acted with no concern.

Tim's laughter stopped, as he ran to his bag of pain. First he removed a small pastry blowtorch. Handing it to Shelly, he said "Light it up...hold it outward...away from you."

She obeyed, holding the shaking flame a distance away. Tim held the iron poker to the red fire. The dark metal turned orange, sizzling on its surface. Small sparks began spitting from it.

Hearing and smelling the evidence, Mike shouted, "What the fuck are you doing?"

Taking his time, Tim made sure it got hotter. Walking back to the tied man, Dr. Abel waved the poker at the drunk driver's face. "Call the cops. I'd write you a letter...but after I burn your eyes out...you won't be able to read it!" he shouted, forcing the hot poker at the douchebag's eye. Mike shut his lid, getting it burned. A high-pitched scream sounded, feeling his lid slowly disintegrate. Tim removed it before touching cornea.

Mike cursed and cried, shouting, "Take whatever the fuck you want! Leave me alone!"

"Oh...I'm going to take exactly what I came here for. I'll take your life...after dismantling you limb from limb. Then...I'll burn you alive."

"You sick fuck!" Mike screamed.

Shelly gasped at Tim's dark words. The vengeful fantasy finally became real. Already disgusted by her uncharacteristic acts of violence, she no longer believed killing was the cure to their pain at all. However, it was too late to turn back.

Tim continued, "Sick? I've been sick for the last ten years, you snot-nosed spoiled fuck!" he yelled, sticking the hot poker on Mike's balls. Although covered, the cloth quickly burned away. Each layer removed, searing pain filled the flailing man. It sizzled testicle skin, branding the drunk's manhood like marked cattle. Tim removed it before burning deeper.

"Ahhhhh! My nuts…my fucking nuts!" he cried out in frantic horror. "I didn't do anything!" He continued shedding tears and screaming.

Aligning his face with the drunk driver, Tim said, "You don't even remember my face."

"I've never seen you before, asshole! You got the wrong fucking man."

"Look at me, you piece of scum!" Tim screamed loudly. His face was red, veins popped from within, spit speckled outwardly.

"Water me down please! I told you, I don't fucking know you!"

"There you were in the courtroom…arrogant smirk on your face…twiddling your fucking thumbs without a care in the world. A man sat across from you…his eyes burning into your soul-less gaze. You looked over once…after the verdict was read, smirking even more. You got away with murder…you got a away with killing my wife!"

The beaten, bloodied man gasped. "You! You're the husband! The dude I wrote the letter to. I apologized for the accident like I had to."

"There was no fucking accident!" Tim screamed, head-butting the punk hard.

Cringing in pain, the guy shouted, "It's not like I meant to kill her."

"You had two DUI's before it! Still…you drove drunk!"

"What do you want from me, asshole? You got the letter!"

A big smile crossed Tim's face. "I want you to suffer…in the exact way I once did."

"How?"

"By denying you what I never had. Your wife and kids will be home in an hour. I'll load them in the car...drive them into a fucking wall!"

Shelly gasped, realizing Tim had lost it. She didn't care about saving Mike's life, it was Tim she had to save from himself. *He's becoming...the thing he hates the most!*

"You piece of shit! My family has nothing to do with this!" Worry and fear painted Mike's face. The arrogance was momentarily lifted from him, clearly hit in his weakest spot.

Rage filled Tim, as he grabbed pictures off the walls. One by one, he held them in Mike's face. The first was a family picture with the kids "Memories!" he shouted, smashing the glass frame the picture was in. Next was a picture of Mike and his wife on the beach, kissing. Tim smashed another one. "Love!" He went on a rampage, smashing every picture they had. "You robbed me of all this!"

"Don't do this, man...please," Mike begged, crying.

"Aww...the scumbag's sad! The scumbag's hurt! Suddenly, when it's his life about to be destroyed, he cries. Do you know how many fucking tears I've cried, you maggot!" he shouted, hurling another fist into Mike's face.

Mike's tears stopped immediately. Clearly, they were false. It was the last straw for Tim Abel. He ran for the gasoline can. Opening the cap, he began soaking his prey to burn alive.

"Help! Someone help me…someone…*GURGLE*…" Tim poured gas into the enemy's mouth. Mike quickly spit it out, gagging up a storm.

Shelly shook in fear, watching in disbelief. In control of the blowtorch, she was the one thing standing between life and death, vengeance and guilt, rationality and rage.

After the can was empty, Tim approached Shelly. Holding out his hand, Tim said, "It's time to end this. It's time to heal our pain."

"This isn't the way, Tim."

"What? You agreed…"

"I thought it would…prayed it would…but all this…healed nothing inside me. Examine your heart…is your pain gone? I hurt every bit as much. He'll get his karma…just not by *our* hands."

Tim paused, feeling the same pain sting his soul. However, he refused to believe it wasn't the answer. In his mind, it was his last chance. "He's not dead yet…we won't know until it's done…until he's a pile of ash."

"No! You sick bastard!" Mike shouted.

Shelly implored Tim, "We can't take this back if we're wrong."

"I can live with that," he said, searching the kitchen cabinets, pulling out drawers. He found what he was seeking. "Matches!" he shouted, holding up the box like a proud father with a newborn.

He removed a match, as Shelly stepped in front of the tied prisoner. "Don't become him, Tim. The moment he dies…we'll become the men who killed our spouses. We'll become the people we hate the most."

"Shelly, I can't live with this pain anymore, regret. I have to make it stop...somehow...someway. If becoming him saves me...then it's a small price to pay," he said, walking past Shelly.

"Just fucking listen to her, bro! I won't tell anyone about this! I swear! Just let me go!"

Tim shoved a nearby cloth napkin into Mike's mouth. "Shut up!"

Her body slumped as she turned her back to the sight. She couldn't watch, hearing Tim strike the match against the box's side. Shelly waited for the sting of hot flames, crackle of snapping fire, scent of burnt flesh, and deathly scream of the drunk driver.

To her surprise, a familiar song filled her ears instead. The sound was nearby, stuck down inside the bag. It was a ringtone from Tim's phone, specific to one caller. A soft trumpet played a calming melody, contrasting the furious situation. *La Vie en Rose*, representing the girl he loved the most.

Holding the flickering flame in-hand, Tim badly needed to end the drunk driver's life. He shamefully felt like Darcy was watching him do it. However, not even *that* could stop him.

"Get ready to burn in hell," Tim said to Mike, letting the matchstick slip from his fingers.

An unexpected voice suddenly made him stop. "Dad?"

To his shock, Tim recaptured the match. He turned to see Shelly holding the phone. She hit speaker, remembering hearing Darcy's ringtone during the therapy session. Knowing the redhead brought light to his life, Shelly took the risk.

"Darcy...I'll have to call you back...I'm in the middle of a heated situation. You're..."

"...Pregnant," Darcy's tearful voice said, hijacking his sentence.

A surreal feeling struck Tim Abel. It was as if his rage suddenly lifted. Even standing there, holding vengeance itself, he nearly forgot about the scumbag in front of him.

"Dad?" Darcy asked again. "Are you OK?"

"I am, baby," he said, his voice breaking up from his own tears. The man began sobbing, uncontrollably. He dropped to his knees. "I *truly* am...my red rose," he said, further breaking down.

Shelly erupted in tears as well, leaning downward, ending the call. She blew out the match in Tim's hand, ensuring he didn't drop it. Shelly asked, "What made you stop?"

"I found it," he said in hysterics. "I finally found it!"

"Found what?"

"The cure...to losing life...losing love."

"Tell me...what is it?" she begged.

"Creating it," he said, gazing deeply in Shelly Cole's eyes.

Without another word spoken, the two lunged for each other. Their tongues danced, hands and faces were speckled with tears and stains of revenge. The drunk driver's swollen eyes watched in disbelief. Soaked in gasoline, cut, bruised, burned and broken, the scumbag wasn't going anywhere.

Still full of adrenaline and aggression, Tim Abel tore at Shelly Cole's clothes. Having created life once *that* night, he ached to do it again. At 40 years of age, the therapist was still fertile. With Darcy as living proof, at 55, Tim's sperm still swam.

Tim tore at the blond's clothes, lifting her shirt above the breasts. Next, he yanked on her bra, freeing a set of D-cups. Like a hungry beast, he gnawed upon tender feminine flesh. He bit a trail downward to rock hard nipples. The doctor switched between teeth and tongue, stimulating Shelly with pain and pleasure.

Having only been with a vibrator in 7 years, the feeling was near magical. Dr. Cole ran her hands through Tim's salt & pepper hair, pushing him further down towards her pussy. Her husband's gift was oral sex, and she'd craved it ever since his death.

Dr. Abel grabbed Shelly's curved hips, licking, biting and sliding down her soft belly. Heading under her skirt, he started from thighs upward again. He began biting upon her soft flesh, giving her pussy chills. With every conquered inch, Tim could smell Shelly's sweet arousal calling him forward. She was so wet, her lust stained white panties.

Arriving at her sweet slit, Tim engulfed the wet cloth with his mouth. Wringing the wet crotch with his lips, Shelly's love juice trickled onto his tastebuds. Using his teeth, he yanked downward. Snapping her waistbands, he tossed Shelly's panties away.

He lunged for her sopping folds. Burying his face within pink satin, he drank Shelly's fine wine. Aged to perfection, he let her feminine juice saturate his mouth. Rising upward, he sucked on her swollen clit. Shelly shook in moments, forced into near instant orgasm. She'd craved it so long, it had been awaiting release.

Dr. Abel pulled his pants down, still fully buckled. His throbbing 8-inches of steel sprang out. The blond therapist reached for it, wrapping her hands upon it like a blind woman touching sight itself. Feeling it again was like rediscovering life.

She led Tim forward, aligning him with her soft hole. He sank inside her creamy red lips. The sensation was surreal to them both. Although Shelly had fingered herself since losing her husband, such length and girth was foreign to her.

Crying out in painful pleasure, she spread her legs in an upward V. Tim rammed all 8-inches inside her at once. They both let out deeply satisfied moans, as if finding an oasis in the desert of life.

It was as if Shelly was Tim's first woman since losing his wife. His balls spanked her thick ass cheeks, her smooth legs wrapped around Tim's muscular ass. He crashed into her with desperate need. It was rough, hard, passionate sex, though it was also loving.

They found the best of both worlds. Shelly moaned with each new impaling. She absorbed every stretching blow, tingling with newfound arousal. The feeling inside her was of lost virginity.

The drunk driver's bloody wounds seeped. Gagged and tied, he was helpless. All he could do was watch his captors fuck. Tim looked up at Mike. It was something much greater than sex to Dr. Abel; it was a declaration of victory. While the drunk took the doctor's life away, it was in his enemy's presence that Tim won it back.

Returning his gaze to Shelly, Tim pounded her hard like a wildling. The blond's tight pussy milked Tim's cock, begging for his cum. She didn't expect to get pregnant at 40, nor was she sure if it'd be wise. Though a part of her needed it.

One hard thrust after another, Tim returned to Shelly's soft lips. With a deep, passionate tongue kiss, he exploded inside the curvy therapist. Breaking the kiss, both cried out in lust. Tim's manly moan was more grunt-like. Shelly's cry was high-pitched, feminine, and tearful. With each load, more salty drops sailed down her cheeks. They weren't tears of sadness, but of joy.

Her legs wrapped tighter around the doctor's ass. Her hands roved his strong, sweat-covered back, feeling his body twitch with every new load. Tim flooded Shelly's sweet pussy. The feeling alone made Shelly shutter in another orgasm. Her tight pussy got tighter, choking every bit of cum from Dr. Abel's thick cock.

Tim's shout echoed through the house. He broke down in tears again. For the first time in a decade, the aching pain of loss was gone. He felt alive. Lowering his head into Shelly's breasts, they both let relief flow like liquid love.

They stayed like that for a good 10 minutes, rising like the reborn. After dressing, they looked over at the gas soaked, battered prisoner. "What are you gonna do with him?" Shelly asked.

Fear danced in Mike's eyes. For the first time ever, the arrogant prick was humbled to the point of real tears. With match in-hand, Tim approached the shaking prisoner. Striking the match on a dry part of Mike's face, Tim waved it in front of him.

The gag was removed, as the drunk driver shouted, "I'm sorry, man! I'm fucking sorry, I really mean it this time. Let me go...I don't wanna die...I'll do anything to save myself. I won't say a word to the cops...I'll tell my wife this was a random robbery. She doesn't even know about my DUI...doesn't know I hit your wife at all!"

"No...you won't tell your wife it was random."

"Why not?"

Tim removed the letter from his pocket. The drunk driver's eyes opened wide, doctor cracked a wicked smile. "Hand me the scalpel," he said to Shelly. Still in a whirl of sex, she retrieved it from the bag, handing it over without question.

"What the hell you gonna do with that?" Mike shouted.

"You won't have to tell your wife what you did," Tim said, placing the court-ordered letter on the drunk driver's shoulder. Dr. Abel plunged the thin blade into it, pinning the letter to his prisoner. "She'll read about it in your own words."

Mike screamed in horrid pain. The doctor knew exactly where to stab, assuring the greatest pain, yet allowing him to live. Tim followed with a hard fist to the head, knocking the enemy unconscious.

"What if he tells?" Shelly asked in worry.

"He won't."

"Why not?"

"Because...he'll never forget me again."

*****

Darcy hugged her stepfather tightly. As awkward as she expected it to be, it wasn't. *It's kinda strange...but I actually feel more comforted, closer to him than ever. I hope he feels the same when I flat out ask him if he knocked me up. I'll do it...nicer than that, of course.*

As the hug broke, a big smile crossed Tim's face. "Congratulations, my red rose."

"You look...different."

"I'm proud."

"Like a father?" she asked, needing an actual confirmation.

He gently nodded, "Like a father," he said passionately.

"I just needed to hear you say it...for sure. But you know...this is Sean's baby. It has to be."

"It is. That's why I did it...for you both. I couldn't be more proud to be a grandfather. I was just the sperm donor...donated a little different than my usual procedure."

Phew, Darcy exhaled. "Thank you for that. Thank you for everything, stepdad." She hugged him again, feeling his love for her. Upon breaking the hug, the same beaming smile stared back. "It's more than pride. That look on your face...in your eyes...it's something else...I can tell."

The newly made man blushed, staring downward. "You know me too well, stepdaughter."

"You met someone."

"She's actually my therapist."

"Isn't that like...illegal?"

"Unethical...not illegal. And let's be honest...who am I to judge ethics?"

"Good point," she said. "So, you're...a couple?"

"We've yet to define it...who knows what the future holds? I just know...I feel alive again. Creating life was the answer. A piece of me...a piece of your mother...via you. It's like...bringing her back," he said. "Balancing the world...with one good soul to offset the bad ones."

A tear rolled down Darcy's cheek. Tim wiped it away, as a tear ran down his own. Darcy did the same to him. "There's one thing I have to ask, stepdad. I'm sorry to do it..."

"I'm going to tell him," he interrupted.

"How'd you know what I was gonna ask?" Darcy asked.

"Because...a family is built on truth...not lies. We owe it to Sean."

Worry painted Darcy's face. "Do you think he'll try to kill us?"

"No."

"You're more confident than I am," she said. "How will you go about it? An alpha thing?"

"No...a family thing."

*****

Tim and Sean Abel sat down at a bar, two beers in-hand. "Cheers," Tim said clinking glasses with his son.

Sean suspiciously clinked back. He watched his father sip the bitter brew. "OK dad, what's wrong?"

"Nothing. Can't a father and son meet for a drink...talk family...family business?"

"You're no drinker...and a bar is as foreign to you as a strip club. Put down the beer and spill your mind."

Tim paused, trying to force the words out. Instead, he sucked down the whole glass of beer. After cringing, he called to the bartender, "I think I need another."

Watching in impressive disbelief, Sean lifted his glass. "After you finally say what you can't seem to say...I may need another as well. Actually, bartender...make it a boilermaker," Sean said, sucking down his glass of beer.

"Make that two boilermakers," Tim joined.

"Uh...dad...not a good idea."

The bartender brought two more beers. He dropped a shot glass of whiskey into the brew. Foaming like a witches' cauldron, it looked quite dangerous to Tim's eyes. He watched Sean drink it straight, catching the shot glass in his mouth afterward.

"You're probably right about *that*, son," he said, pushing the drink away.

"Come on, dad...just spit it out already."

After another long nervous pause, Tim quickly blurted out, "I impregnated Darcy." Panic filled him, as he felt like a son about to be punished. Unable to look at Sean's reaction, Tim grabbed the boilermaker, sucking down the strong brew. Catching the cup in his mouth, he gagged the glass back into the mug. "My God! What's wrong with you? Drinking that poison?"

Sean smirked. "Now that's the father I recognize."

Tim was shocked. He expected his son to go on a rampage. "Did you hear what I said *before* the drink? I *seeded* her!"

"I heard what you said...and I already knew."

"Darcy told you? You're not fuming at the mouth? I drugged..."

Sean held up his hand, "I don't wanna know any damn details. I'd prefer to picture a test-tube...nothing more."

"I can gladly omit details."

"Darcy told me."

"I told her I'd confess."

"She didn't tell me about you...her pregnancy."

"Then what did she tell you?"

Sean paused, thinking back to Darcy's words. "She told me about a certain day...months ago. She found you standing at a gravestone."

"It feels like just yesterday."

"You who told her, 'You belong with a Dr. Abel...just not me.' You told her...we deserved to be together...she belonged with me...not you."

"And I was right, son. I let *my* pain, *my* hurt, *my* selfishness cloud my fatherly judgment. I failed you during those days. And to be honest, I feared I might've failed you now."

"But you got it right in the end...*then* and *now*. Am I happy I couldn't knock up my wife? No. But I'm grateful you risked everything...to help us."

"I did. I love you both...willing to do anything to save you...from the life and pain I lived. Tell me though, honestly...how'd you really know?"

"I'm a doctor, dad."

"And a damn good one...in case I haven't told you before."

Sean was shocked, having never heard his father say it. The senior doctor was hard on Sean throughout, intent on making his son the best doctor he could be. "Well, I may not be an OBGYN...T," Sean smirked, "But I've given my share of disappointing diagnosis. Incurable cancer, rare diseases...so on. When you called with the news...your tone said it all. It *was* my fault."

"Son, it's not a case of fault! It's a case of biology...nothing you could do!"

"I know...I know. I also know...you were trying to protect me from my macho-self...an impossible task. You wanna know the truth? If I had to choose anyone's sperm to fill in for mine...you'd be the man."

A humbled Tim hugged his son. As the hug broke, Tim yelled, "Bartender, two more boilermakers."

"Dad?"

"What the hell…you only live once."

*****

9 Months Later

A full-term, round-bellied Darcy waddled into her stepfather's exam room. Sean accompanied her. The redhead changed into her gown, sitting in the chair. Having carried full-term, she was expected to go into labor at any moment.

"Let's do it," Sean said with a devious look in his eyes.

"What? Here? Now? Stepdad can walk in on us!" Darcy exclaimed.

"Has any doctor ever come in immediately? Trust me…we take our time."

She paused, having been extra horny during her gestational period. "I may regret this…but…take me!" she said, giving in to raging hormones.

"Just like we pretended…on our honeymoon," Sean said, snapping on rubber gloves. "But this fantasy…will come true." He lowered the gyno chair. Darcy's back lay flat, her feet were raised in stirrups. The redhead's gown fell open, swollen pregnant belly and breasts heaved upward towards the heavens. Her red pubic hair had grown back in full, fiery as a burning bush. Legs spread wide, the patient's pink slit was on full display.

Stepbrother Sean removed his clothes, revealing cut abs, strong legs and arms, a model-like body. The dark-haired doctor put on a white medical jacket. He followed by administering the stethoscope to his neck. His 7-inch cock protruded from the coat's open part, pointing right for her pussy. He inhaled, following Darcy's arousal home.

Sliding his cock along her slit, he entered with ease. The exam room door suddenly opened. Darcy gasped.

It was Dr. Tim Abel. He let out a gasp as well. "I'm sorry," he said, turning to leave.

"No, Dad…stay," Sean said.

"Excuse me?" Tim asked.

"Yeah…excuse you?" Darcy questioned in shock.

"She belongs to us both...at least...one *last* time," he said with sincerity in his voice. "We'll examine her...in every intimate way."

Darcy and her stepfather shared shocked gazes. Without a word spoken, Tim frantically removed his clothes. Also opting to keep on his jacket only, his 8-inch cock sprang out of it. He snapped on gloves too, approaching his pregnant stepdaughter with lustful desire.

Oh shit! It's just like what I imagined on our wedding night...in my head! Darcy thought.

Dr. Tim Abel removed the medical tape, wrapping his stepdaughter's wrists. Tossed to Sean, the younger doctor taped his stepsister's ankles. Stepfather Tim went straight for Darcy's mouth. His manly arrow aimed for her lips. She opened on command, swallowing his thick rod. Offering no pause, he sank into an immediate deep throat. The pregnant redhead took every inch without a single gag, thanks to stepfather's expert teaching.

Sean watched his father's eyes roll upward in pleasure, as he fucked Darcy's soft mouth. The stepbrother drove into his stepsister's pussy, holding onto her thick thighs. He pounded her, balls-deep. Dual sensations tingled Darcy's body.

The senior doctor roved Darcy's breasts with a latex touch. Over the 9 months, they swelled from C-cup to D. His large expert hands massaged and squeezed the massive mammaries like water balloons. Suddenly, he reached over to the nearby drawer. With cock remaining in stepdaughter's mouth, he removed two small rubber bands and two forceps clamps. Although the bands were often used for hemorrhoid tying, it was clear Dr. Abel had something different in mind.

Tossing one to Sean, father and son stretched the medical bands around Darcy's breasts. Then, they twisted the ends so they bubbled, growing another cup size. Pausing a moment, Darcy freed her mouth, moaning from the pressure. Tim grabbed a handful of red hair, forcing her mouth back onto his slippery throbbing cock.

With both medical bands in place, they clamped Darcy's puffed aureoles. The forceps' mouths clamped from the sides. Darcy moaned in painful pleasure, feeling like her breasts would explode. Sensitive nerves within the nipple were stimulated, milk ducts were primed. It was milk Tim had a craving for.

Stepfather Tim Abel grabbed a nipple, beginning a tugging motion. His face tightened, feeling his stepdaughter's mouth tighten around his thick cock. Sean reached for the opposite nipple, jerking it even harder. Darcy's pussy also tightened, making Sean grit his teeth.

The pregnant redhead moaned through the cock gag. Both men fucked her holes harder, milking her nipples more aggressively. They kept it up, fighting their own releases, eager to free the expecting mother of her breast milk. Their latex pinch combined with the rubber bands and clamps. Darcy's breasts turned a slight shade of purple, red tips tingled with fire.

A tiny droplet of clear liquid appeared, proving they'd struck gestational gold. Tim Abel positioned his head down to Darcy's engorged breasts. Wanting to taste his wife, Sean leaned in to suck the other. They drank the rising liquid like concrete through straws.

The men bit on the tender tips like rare prime rib. Soon, ecstasy seeped from her nipple like a calcium fountain.

Darcy wanted to shout, feeling stinging pressure tingle her tits. However, she was forced to accept more of her stepfather and stepbrother. A breast induced orgasm trickled through her body. Although not quite as powerful as a vaginal or clitoral explosion, it teased her just right.

Having drank their fill of their step-kin, the men returned to upright positions. With one hand pumping Darcy's red hair, Tim gently grabbed his stepdaughter's throat, removing it just as quick.

"Choke her," Sean said, handing over the stethoscope to his father.

"She's pregnant…it's…not a very good…"

"She wants this…*badly*," he said.

Darcy's head bobbed in agreement, still sucking away at her stepfather's hard cock. Tim excitingly wrapped the cord around her tender neck. Starting aggressively, he pulled hard, restricting air from her windpipe. Darcy immediately felt the pressure build in her head. Tim was impressed that his stepdaughter went from an inexperienced virgin to sexual freak in mere months.

His squeeze got harder, as Darcy's mouth opened, gasping desperately for air. He quickly gagged her deeper with a bulbous head. Sailing across her flailing tongue, he plugged her throat.

Sean continued driving into his stepsister's soaked pussy. Her sweet juices were spackled all over his balls and thighs, running down his muscular legs. He watched Darcy's face match her hair, beet red. The step-doctor got more aroused seeing his wife's arms and legs struggle to break free of her tape-bond. He knew dark pleasure was accompanying it.

Stepfather and stepbrother pounded away with alpha vigor, fucking Darcy's mouth and pussy. A fan of sexual asphyxiation anyway, Darcy's pregnant hormones increased the taboo pleasure. The more she gasped, the tighter Tim choked her with the stethoscope.

Finally, Darcy broke. Her curved body shook in captivity, grinding into the reclined gyno seat. Both her pussy and mouth tightened around the dual step-cocks. She felt her stepfather's balls smack her face, stepbrother's balls smack her curvy ass. Dizzy flutters filled Darcy's mind, rounded body heaved in fits of electric orgasm.

Pushed to the edge of consciousness, her pleasure was heightened when both men erupted inside her. Stepfather erupted first, firing a hot load into her warm wet mouth. The sweet and savory seed sailed into her throat, flooding so furiously, she could barely swallow it fast enough.

Then came the gush of stepbrother sperm into Darcy's pregnant pussy. Although not as virile as his father's, Sean's delivery was fuller. He kept firing like a cum cannon, his stepsister was the battlefield.

Filled from both ends, Darcy lay captive to their dominance. The young girl basked in sacred submission to the men she loved. After firing their last loads, they withdrew. A white ring remained around both sets of feminine lips.

Darcy's luscious, life-filled curves swayed with the entrance of each step-offering. Her body was pushed beyond physical, emotional, and mental limits. One moment it was harsh pain, then unreal pleasure. Her G-spot was squashed by two cocks, vaginal and anal nerves stimulated on and off.

Tim and Sean Abel's faces tensed in sexual anguish. Their joint invasion crowded every inch of the pregnant patient. The tightness nearly burst their cocks. As Darcy placed her hands on stepfather Tim's white-coated chest, she rocked back and forth, shifting her full body weight. Each cock was milked to a straining point.

Feeling cum rise, both men couldn't fight it anymore. Sean was the first to erupt inside his stepsister's ass. Streams of hot cum coated Darcy's anal avenue. The sticky, squishy inner-feeling pushed her further off the sexual cliff.

Next, stepfather Tim blasted his stepdaughter's pussy with a life-giving load. Yet again, Darcy was cream-filled in two orifices by her step-doctors. Suddenly, a shout escaped her, entire body shifting and shaking like the deepest quake.

Every curve on her trembled, breath huffed and puffed. She'd never felt such a pleasure-rush strike her at once. It was like every orgasm she'd ever had, combined into one tidal wave.

Her body pushed so hard, she squirted G-spot fluid all over her stepfather's cock. In the midst of squirting one end, her swollen strained nipples fired another type of squirt. New streams of breast milk baptized stepfather Tim's chest and face.

As her last wave of orgasm swept over, Darcy crashed upon her stepfather, Sean sandwiched her. After a moment of sweaty quiet, she started moaning again. "Another orgasm?" Sean asked, realizing her cry sounded different.

"No...Sean...I think I'm having the baby! Like...right now!"

"The sex...induced her!" Tim realized. "Her water must've broke with the squirt! Couldn't have happened in a better place."

"Or with a better doctor. Are you ready to deliver my child, Dr. Abel?" Sean said, as both men withdrew from Darcy's holes.

"I'm ready," Tim said with conviction.

"Then to the hospital we go."

*****

"It's a girl!" Dr. Tim Abel shouted, holding up a healthy child. The umbilical cord was cut. Dried and nasally squeegeed, she was placed in Darcy's arms. The redhead cried as her stepbrother and stepfather joined her in joy.

"She's amazing!" Sean declared. "I just realized we never discussed names."

Both Darcy and Tim connected gazes. "*Debra* Abel," they jointly announced, honoring the woman taken from them years ago. Tim's pain was not only gone, but for the first time since losing his wife, his heart was officially healed.

"I want you to meet someone," Tim said, motioning his nurse to bring someone in.

Everyone waited in wonderment. Shelly Cole entered, her warm smile greeting them all. "Hello," she said. "I'm Shelly, nice to meet you both."

"The *therapist*," Darcy said.

"Yes," Tim told her. "Though now...you can call her...my woman," he said in pride.

"Actually...there's a new title," Shelly informed him.

"Really?" Tim asked in surprise. "What is it?"

"Baby-mama," Shelly said with a smirk.

Greater shock filled Tim's face. "You're pregnant? We did it?"

"We did," she said, finally free from her own pain. For the first time, she also found the cure to losing love, losing life. It was giving birth to new love, new life.

"Come on, everyone...a hug," Tim said, all four embraced around the new child.

"Here's to step-family," Darcy said.

"No." Tim corrected her. "Here's to family."

Other Books by J.D. Grayson

More titles available on Amazon

All books are now available in Paperback. For autographed copies please send your request to JDGrayson@hotmail.com

THE STEP DOCTORS
Available at: Amazon

Darcy Smith enters her stepfather's medical practice. Expecting to see the usual female physician, Dr. Sean Abel arrives instead. The 30 year-old stepbrother dares to break his father's rule, forbidden from examining the girl. Thrust into a living-taboo, the step-doctor intimately explores the girl he was raised with.

Learning of the insubordination, Dr. Tim Abel disciplines his son. However, the stepfather questions his own hidden fantasies, enticing him to break his own rules. As Darcy comes to enjoy it, an unthinkable decision arises. Could she fall in love with her step-doctors? More importantly, could she actually choose between the two of them?

*****

YOUR FRIENDLY NEIGHBORHOOD BDSM CLUB
Available at: Amazon

After entering the local PTA meeting, Caroline Chase feels out of place. She finds an unwelcoming bunch of ladies, prim and proper in every manner. Owen Hayes, the dapper PTA president, presents the same air of perfection. Too good to be true, she knows the most polished people often hide the dirtiest secrets.

Intrigued by the group's plastic facade, Caroline Chase returns again. It's then, she finds a reality which only existed in her sexual fantasies. Challenged to submit, she'll be forced to face questions of inner strength and willpower. However, Caroline will soon discover, she's not the only one in need of an awakening.

*****

THE PREGNANCY TRANCE
Available at: Amazon

Amber Evans enters a hypnotherapist's office seeking help. Unable to get pregnant, she's desperate to find an answer. Eager to cure her, Bruce Carson examines her subconscious mind, treading a darker path than he expected to walk.

Fighting his own battle of darkness, Bruce hopes redemption lies in Amber's cure. Though to heal her, he'll have to survive the dangerous place it takes him. Obsessed with his mission, he'll even risk his life to deliver the pregnancy trance.

*****

MARRIAGE THERAPY:
A DOM, A SUB & A CUCKOLD
Available at: Amazon

Lori and Tyler Hale have a nice home, good jobs, and decent relationship. Though while Tyler is happy to forego bedroom matters, Lori desires a kinky edge. With no answer in sight, the couple turns to marriage therapy.

Recommended by a friend, Dr. Stone welcomes the couple into his office. The Hales soon discover their therapist's unique way of treatment. Using the tools of sexual discipline, he pushes their marriage to the edge. Willing to risk their breaking, he challenges their sexual limits. Though the more he explores his female patient, the more he's tempted to let them fail.

*****

THE FANTASY FACTORY: EDGY ROLE PLAY
Available at: Amazon

Vicky Lane's sex life has hit a wall. Failing to spice things up with sexy outfits and toys, the luscious housewife threatens her husband with an affair. After he carelessly dares her to go forward, Vicky calls Gavin's bluff. Raising the stakes, she lets her dark side shine.

She signs up for the fantasy factory, where fantasy becomes reality. Wanting to act out her darkest taboo, she signs her freedom away, putting it in the hands of unknown men. Taken at random, an edgy adventure follows suit. Vicky hopes to teach Gavin a lesson of her value, though by the end, the lesson will belong to them both.

The Fantasy Factory series will be an occasional series of non-sequential, "Paid for hire" role-play. They can be read in any order.

*****

DOCTOR MÉNAGE
Available at: Amazon

Returning to their hometown in style, Doctors Mason & Ross open a sexual medicine practice. Blessed with wealth and good looks, the bachelors are desired by every female in the zip code. Since the girls can't win the doctors' hearts, they must settle for sexual treatment instead.

Attending their high-school reunion, the doctors are approached by a face from their past. The popular and beautiful Kayla Carter seeks them out, hoping they'll cure her sexual dysfunction. Agreeing to treat her, the two doctors make a deal to stimulate her body, but not their hearts. Of course, promises are easier to make than keep.

*****

THE COLONY:
ARRIVAL (PART I)
TEMPTATION (PART II)
PROPHECY (PART III)
ADDICTS (PART IV)
Available at: Amazon, Smashwords, iBooks & B&N

After years of marital heartache, Dylan & Alexa Hunter have lost the will to go on. After being approached by a mysterious man, they are offered a chance to start over in a utopian paradise. The word eternity is spoken, though left undefined.

On the island of Aionios, no fruit is forbidden, no pleasure denied. Accepting the tempting offer, the couple surrenders everything, including freewill itself. Though they'll soon learn that even paradise has a dark side.

*****

SLAVES & BREEDERS:
ABDUCTED INTO SEX SLAVERY (PART I)
CHOSEN TO BREED (PART II)
INTO THE FIRE (PART III)
Available at: Smashwords, iBooks & B&N

Having grown up in foster care, Haley White only knows disappointment. Cloaked in a mask of false strength, the troubled teen enters a world of harsh reality. As she attempts to better her life, few opportunities open their door to her.

As the years tick by, the 21-year old discovers an ad for a modeling agency. Tired of working small jobs for small money, she agrees to a photo shoot. After being chosen for the position, her fate takes a frightening turn. Haley White is abducted.

Taken to a remote island, she's an immediate candidate to breed her new master's heir. However, her rebellious attitude will have to be broken first. Feeling helpless in her captivity, she finds that her captor shares a common bond.

*****

THE PATIENT:
PHYSICAL (PART I)
DOUBLE DOSE (PART II)
THE CURE (PART III)
Available at: Amazon, B&N, iBooks, Smashwords, KOBO, Sony, and Diesel

Twenty-two year old, Rebecca Stone is a naive girl with medical anxiety. Having minimal sexual experience, and being submissive in nature, she is prime meat in the hands of horny predators. Sensing her obvious weakness, her new boss demands a pre-employment physical. However, what she doesn't know, is that the doctor's secretly working with him, exploiting timid girls like herself.

Rebecca is forced to face her deep fear of doctors, pulled into a world of medical submission. Along the journey, she will discover the root of her feelings, and gain a newfound fetish in the process.

*****

TEACHING EMMA:
A CONTRACT OF SUBMISSION (PART I)
THE MASTER/SUB EXPERIENCE (PART II)
FREEDOM OF SUBMISSION (PART III)
Available at: Amazon, Smashwords, iBooks & B&N

Emma Heart starts college with an unusual elective: Human Sexuality-Fetish and Lifestyles. She doesn't know that her new teacher, Mark Ryan, is as unusual as the course itself. The class is given a contract of submission, agreeing to become his subs, empowering him their Dom. The lessons that follow will not be learned from books, but bodies.

As he focuses on Emma, Professor Ryan begins to question his own methods. Feeling stronger for his student than expected, he realizes the only outcome is heartbreak. He must decide between love or scholastic duty. The question is...can he?

*****

THE HYPNOTIST: SEX TRANCE
Available at: Amazon

Hoping to cure his wife's bedroom boredom, Sean Day turns to hypnotherapist, Joseph Ryan, to cure his wife. Though, due to Misty's uptight upbringing, the hypnotist is forced to skirt the rules. He lies to her.

Under the guise of smoking addiction treatment, Misty is seduced into trance. Joseph intends to fix her intimacy issues. However, after exploring Misty's dark mind, a deeper issue is revealed. Her words unlock Mr. Ryan's own unspoken fetish, forcing him to break new ground. Pushed to the edge of submission, Mrs. Day will face her shameful secrets, along with the mental bonds that hold her captive.

*****

THE DENTIST: SEDATION
Available at: Amazon

Throughout Dr. Ivy's life, a dark fantasy has tested his limits of self-control. Finally ready to cross the threshold of reality, the allure of exploiting sedated patients claims him. As satisfying as the experience turns out, it fails to cure a lonely heart.

Realizing he requires more than a warm body, the doctor revisits an abandoned idea. Working on numerous formulas, he discovers that the right mix of nitrous oxide will make his dream come true.

Just when his plans are in place, a new regulation forces him to hire a dental assistant. The beautiful Kimberly Carter arrives, watching his every move. It appears his fantasy-driven dreams are thwarted, when he discovers his assistant may share them as well.

About J.D. Grayson

All books are now available in Paperback. For autographed copies please send your request to JDGrayson@hotmail.com

Website: www.JDGraysonBooks.com
Twitter: @JDGraysonBooks
Facebook: http://www.facebook.com/JDGraysonBooks

You can contact J.D. Grayson at JDGrayson@hotmail.com

J.D. Grayson lives in the state of Florida, where the heat and sweat naturally lead him to write erotica. Preferring short erotica to long form, he tries to offer a burst of pleasure, while merging an interesting story with a few twists along the journey.

With every work, Grayson attempts to straddle the line of sensuality and kink, story and sex, as well as fantasy and reality. Although sex always leads the way, he strives to add imagination to every plot line, in addition to each sex act. Some stories are lighter in tone; others are darker, though he always aims for a tasteful presentation.

His ultimate goal is to add spice to the life of readers. In his daily conversations with "average couples," he discovered that the current state of sexuality is not in a good place. Somehow, it's been lost in maddening schedules, busy lives, and shamed stereotypes. Its importance and priority are pushed to the back burner, as a chore not a reliever.

If just one of his stories adds some lust to their love, then his mission is accomplished.

www.ingramcontent.com/pod-product-compliance
Lightning Source LLC
Chambersburg PA
CBHW022005170626
46808CB00001B/297